OTHER BOOKS BY
BRENDA JOYCE NICHOLS

Journal Your Personal Testimonies

Heaven Must Be Like This

Heavenly Portions

Blind But Now I See (Living with Keratoconus)

Passion & Purpose Workbook

22 Wisdom Keys
(Reflections of a Modern Day Proverb 31 Wife)

A Husband to Call My Own

A NOVEL
Choosing Abstinence

Brenda Joyce Nichols

This is a work of romantic fiction with a foundation of biblical truths. The characters are men and women of faith striving to live God's way!

———————————

———————————

———————————

Cover Design - Brenda Joyce Nichols
Logo Design - Pam McFarland

———————————

Breicha Publishing Company
Memphis, TN 38134
Website: www.brendajoycenichols.com
Email: brenda@brendajoycenichols.com

A Husband To Call My Own

Dear Reader,

In 2006, I wrote this book and put it away. In 2015, I was looking for a good novel to read. It was awesome how the Holy Spirit led me to read my unfinished manuscript.

"Lord, can I publish it?" was my first thought.

"Sure, I've given you the desires of your heart to write novels," came the response from deep within.

I've learned that in most fiction novels there are elements of truth. Many of us share similar testimonies and God wants us to give witness to how He provides a way out — no matter what the temptation or circumstance.

It's my prayer that this literary work will bring liberty to those who are bound in adulterous affairs and promiscuous lifestyles. It is my prayer that the message in this novel will be a fresh and creative way to bring hope, encouragement, and a way of escape.

Enjoy the story and discuss the questions found in the back. It will be an easy read that can bring truth and liberation to your situation and matters of the heart — if you follow the biblical principles.

"No temptation has overtaken you that is not common to man. God is faithful, and he will not let you be tempted beyond your ability, but with the temptation he will also provide the way of escape, that you may be able to endure it." (1 Corinthians 10:13 ESV)

Always In His Service,
Brenda Joyce Nichols

Acknowledgments

I thank God for the life changing experience that serves as a foundational base for this novel. I thank God for others who have shared their experiences to confirm how God provides a way of escape when we turn to Him.

I acknowledge my husband, Reggie, whom God provided as my way of escape thirty-six years ago. Together, we entered into holy matrimony as new creations in Him. And, it is Him who bonded us and keeps us today.

I acknowledge our children, Carlos, Roslyn, Reggie Edward, and Ryan. God blessed and our quiver is full with two daughters-in-law, six grandchildren, and one great-grandson. Oh my, God blessed us indeed!

I acknowledge my biological sisters Lillie Plunkett and Barbara Miller, who have nurtured me unconditionally then and now. And, two very special sistah-girls, Marie Gillespie and Odell Owens, who've walked up-close-and-personal in various seasons of my life.

I acknowledge my Sisters-in-Christ, whom God has put in my life for Kingdom purposes; Rev. Dr. Earnestine Hunt, Apostle Catherine Burks, and Evangelist Tonya Taylor. A special thanks to Jeanna Brandon, Liza Royal, and Joyce Mason for reading and providing feedback while in manuscript status. More thanks to my Mt. Zion Baptist Church family, Theresa Thornton, and the Women's Ministry of the Pentecostal Baptist Church in Memphis, TN for embracing me in such a supportive way.

I thank the readers who have encouraged and supported my literary endeavors. Especially those who are still waiting for book three of *Heaven Must Be Like This* and *Heavenly Portions*. As always and I'm still saying, "it's coming!"

Lastly, I thank each of you that will read this novel and share its message to the world. *To God Be The Glory!*

Dedication

Emma Delores "Lois" Williams
Rest-in-Heaven, our dear sister
(1951-1999)

Shouts of praise filled the church as Pastor Kenton ended his Wednesday night sermon. The choir went into high praise when he extended the invitation to discipleship. As usual, no one joined on Wednesday  nights—except for Mack Earl, the local neighborhood drunk. Every Wednesday night, he would walk down the aisle and confess that he was born again. Patiently, Pastor Kenton would take his hand and keep him at his side.

"Why don't they do something about that man," Serena exclaimed, stepping out of her choir robe. "He is a complete nuisance to this church."

"Don't be so hard on him," a choir member laughed. "He's just getting his church on."

"Well, someone should talk to him and explain church etiquette," Serena stated firmly.

"Now that is something the whole church needs," another voice chimed in. "And since you're so prim and proper, you should teach it!"

Laughter and giggling quickly filled the room of teens and a few adults, which made up the small choir.

Serena Garrett had attended Faith Baptist Church all of her life. Her parents lived right across the street from the church and had kept a key to the church since she was a toddler. When her father retired he took on the title of Custodial Engineer as Pastor Kenton had gladly announced.

"Clear the church, clear the church," Samuel Garrett announced. "It's time to lock up. I ain't coming back through here to referee no fight between faithful, dedicated, Christian folks."

Serena quietly shut her mouth and moved around the snickering choir members and headed out the door.

"Serena, go on over to the house and get your supper on the stove," her father's voice trailed behind her. "Your Mama been keeping that plate warm all evening for you."

Serena rushed out the door and on to the parking lot. She welcomed the warm summer night air.

"Hey Serena," her best friend, Dimples, shouted out. "Are you going with us tonight?"

Serena didn't respond and kept a steady pace to her car. All she wanted was to hurry home to her apartment to enjoy a nice warm bubble bath. She didn't know why she stayed so faithful and loyal to this church. The people were small-minded and no matter how much teaching Pastor Kenton provided, they just didn't seem to be growing to a spiritual maturity to her liking.

Serena switched on the ignition and put the car in reverse. She barely missed backing into Mack Earl, who was engaged in his usual solicitation for some pocket change.

"Take it easy Miss Lady," he shouted towards her. "You trying to run down a true saint of God or something? A brother just trying to get some money for a tall cold can of nourishment."

Just about that time, Dimples stuck her head in the passenger side of the open window, startling her noticeably agitated and upset friend.

"Girl, what's up? "You've been on edge lately."

Dimples got into the car and settled into the passenger's seat. She was holding onto a plate of turnip greens, tomato and cucumber salad, baked chicken, cornbread, and apple cobbler.

"Slow your roll. I don't want to spill this plate your Mama sent to you. Something ain't right! We need to talk!"

Serena averted her gaze and shifted into another gear. "Do you need a ride home or something?" she asked hastily. "Don't you need to be leaving with your so called partying, saved, and sanctified friends?"

"I'm riding with you! Plus, you know you're my for real so called saved and sanctified friend," Dimples replied sarcastically. "I think you need me more than they do."

"Dimples, all I need is to go home and be by myself. I don't need you and nobody else prying into my business."

"I think you do," Dimples shouted back. "Serena, for the last few months you've had one bad attitude. Girl, we need to pray them demons out of you. I promised your Mama that I would get to the bottom of whatever it is that has turned you into Sister Killjoy."

Serena's thoughts were racing. She didn't want to take her frustrations out on Dimples and the people who cared about her. She was living a shameful and sinful lie and couldn't tell anyone. Who could she tell? Who could help her? Nobody!

"What difference does it make?" Serena snapped. "We're all going to hell. We're all just a bunch of hypocrites. Lost and hell-bound. And Dimples, you of all people should be the last person trying to give out some Christian advice."

"Oh my, this is going to be a biggie," Dimples sighed, buckling her seat belt. "This is going to call for much patience and prayer."

Serena could hardly hold back the burning tears that had begun to roll softly down her cheeks. "Dimples, I'm taking you home because this is not a night for me to have overnight guest."

Dimples' heart was troubled for her friend. What had happened to Serena? Why was she slipping more and more away from her? She desperately wanted to help her in some way–but how? She had hoped that Serena would open up to her. She knew parts of her truth, but obviously it was more involved than what Serena was sharing.

"Well, take me home because I didn't drive my car tonight," Dimples insisted. "I'm not giving up and we will visit this subject again. Now do us both a favor, and dry your face of those big crocodile tears, so you can at least see where we're going before you kill us both."

"Thanks Dimples," Serena wiped her tear-stricken face. "Just be patient with me. I'm going to need you and every prayer warrior that can get a prayer through to heaven before this is over."

Serena shifted the gears of her well used Camry and drove off the church's parking lot. She knew she needed to talk to somebody. She'd kept her secret long enough. She'd been telling only half-truths to Dimples. She'd lied to her parents and coworkers. She was lying to herself. Truth be told, she was even lying to God.

Serena Rachel Garrett stared at her reflection in the mirror. "Girl, how could you let this go on for four years?" she asked the reflection staring back. "Don't you know that you're just another one of his trophies?"

Serena looked at her reflection and spoke back to her conscience. It was the one and only voice that knew and condemned her sins of secrecy and adultery. "I can't do this much longer. I'm dying within myself," she sighed heavily.

She didn't like the image staring back at her anymore. She could no longer see the attractive, bubbly personality, and outgoing person that had once occupied her body. What she saw were eyes that cried themselves to sleep every night. Shadows of sadness and loneliness had replaced the twinkle and shine in her soft brown eyes and a smile that no longer brightened her face. There was no innocence of a true and godly love with someone who could love her back.

Her four year affair with Edgar Dupree was not at all what she had wanted to happen. But, like so many other lonely and single women, she stepped into Satan's trap, closed her eyes, and allowed herself to fall in love with a married man.

"End it now…you have to make a choice," her voice of reason whispered back. "I know….my soul is at risk," she answered silently, turning away from the all-knowing mirror of her mind. "This has got to end," she cried out. "I've got to choose—it's life or death!"

Lost in her thoughts, she opened the closet door and hung up her peach summer blouse and ivory colored linen slacks. She put on a pair of freshly washed sweats and an oversized tee-shirt. There was no need to slip into a soft lacey nightgown on tonight. There would be no preparation for a lover's bed. There would be no love songs playing softly in the background. There was no indication that the evening promised its usual atmosphere of romance and lovemaking. In her mind, the only sounds of passion filling the room would be the deep soul wrenching dialogue of a lover's paradise coming to an end.

She brushed down the curls of her short stylish haircut and removed all traces of makeup from her face. "I choose life and not death! No longer will my bedroom, body, mind, or spirit continue down this path!" she spoke loudly.

With a newfound strength and determination, she closed the door to her bedroom. She felt bold, confident, and strong. Although Edgar had his own key to her apartment, he always rang the doorbell and gave his familiar offbeat knocks before opening the door. On tonight, his entrance into her convenient and cozy apartment would bring deliverance and redemption for both of their soul's sake.

About an hour later, Edgar's disappointed voice came over the telephone. "I'm sorry baby, I'm on an all-nighter. I'll make it up to you this weekend."

"I was expecting to see you tonight," Serena sighed heavily. "Remember, Wednesday is my night."

"Look baby, we're going to change that because you're not in the right mood after you leave church. We end up wasting time that I don't have. I'll stop by to see you at your desk before you leave work tomorrow."

Serena didn't have the desire to persuade him to come over. Although, in her mind she was ready to end the affair, she didn't trust her heart.

"Come on and tell me what I want to hear," Edgar whispered.

"I love you," Serena stated softly.

"Who's your man? Who do you belong too?"

"I belong to you," she sighed.

"That's right and don't you ever forget it," he laughed.

Instead of sleeping, Serena thought back on how she'd fallen into the devil's pit by getting involved with Edgar Dupree.

She was on the way home from her night classes at the university when the tire on her Camry blew out on the interstate. She held the car steady until it swerved off the road. Edgar Dupree was going in the opposite direction. He noticed the distressed motorist and got off at the next exit to return and help.

Serena was unhurt and standing next to her car assessing the damage when he pulled up. They both realized that they worked in the same building and had seen each other in passing. She didn't have a spare tire. He took full control of the situation and took her home after the car was towed. She was a Secretary in the City's public transit department, and he was in a division of law enforcement that was two floors above her. At the time, he was separated from his wife, with three children, and he claimed that reconciliation was not in their future.

She had fallen instantly in love with his style, charm, and captivating personality. He was twelve years her senior, medium frame, with a full head of shortly cropped hair. His mustache was always trimmed and he was an impeccable dresser. He stood just four inches taller than her five feet five inch frame. His medium built, muscular body, was firm and fit. His warm brown skin coloring complimented his eyes.

It was his eyes that had looked deep down inside her. He touched a place in her heart that no man had ever touched in her life. He knew how to make her laugh, smile, and could word her thoughts, feelings, hopes, and dreams better than she could herself.

From the very beginning, she had known that he was married, but their friendship had continued to grow at the office. First, it was catching a quick lunch together or he would bring lunch to her desk. When his work schedule would change, she would meet him for dinner, or at an after work spot. Her weekends became filled with his phone calls and constant attention when he wasn't on special assignment or out-of-town. With work, school, church, and being with Edgar, her life was blissfully full.

One year later, and on her 25th birthday, Serena received her undergraduate's degree in Psychology. Her parents, Samuel and Gladys Garrett, were so very proud of her. She hated the lies she told them about dating and not being able to meet the right man. She was their only child and they were anxiously awaiting a few grandchildren to adore and love.

"Oh Serena, you're the best thing that God gave us," her mother cried on her graduation day. "So hurry and give us a grandbaby before we get to old."

Serena's heart broke into a thousand pieces every time her parents mentioned grandchildren. She knew the best gift she could ever give them would be a son-in-law and grandchildren. What her parents didn't know and what she couldn't tell them was that the man she was in love with was married and grandchildren were not likely to happen anytime soon.

"Maybe, that man she's been hiding will soon put a ring on her finger," her father laughed. "Let's just give her the keys to this new car. Maybe, one day she'll give us some babies now that she's on her way to settling down."

Sam handed Serena a set of keys to a new Mercedes that was parked directly in front of them. Sam and Gladys watched with excitement as their baby girl screamed with joy. Serena was overwhelmed with tears as she hugged her parents.

"You've worked hard to be on your own and get your education," her mother stated. "Enjoy this gift that we have wanted to give you for a very long time."

Later that night, Edgar gave her a heart-shaped diamond necklace to pledge his love and devotion. And, just a few days later, he gave her the saddest news that her heart could bear. He told her that he was moving back home with his wife and children.

"I have no choice," he pleaded with Serena. "She doesn't want a divorce. She still thinks that we can reconcile. We got married too young. We were both eighteen when she got pregnant. I did the right thing and I've got to keep on doing the right things for their welfare."

Serena could feel her heart breaking into a thousand pieces. She had given him her heart. She had thrown all logic and sense out the window when it came to loving him. She had walked into this relationship with her eyes wide opened and now it had come to this.

Edgar continued to pour out his situation. "Babycakes, she needs me, and the children need me. They're depending on me for everything. They can't make it without me financially. I went on and developed my career, but she didn't because of the children. Serena, sweetheart, I promise when my youngest comes out of high school, we'll be together. She's trying to get herself together and live independent of me. I just can't leave them right now. Babycakes, please wait for me. One day we will be together. I need you to just wait for me…wait for me to be free."

He sobbed hopelessly in her arms. From that night on they shared their deepest thoughts and dreams to each other. Serena had found a love that she had never felt for a man and a love that she wanted no matter the cost. She lived and breathed for the stolen time that they spent together. His touch and kisses sent her to places she had never been. It was easy surrendering to him. She gave him her heart, body, and soul.

She had settled for being second and never being seen with him in public, unless they were in the company of others. She had settled for dropping everything she was doing on a moment's notice to come and go, whenever he traveled out of the city, and requested her company. She had settled for spending holidays and weekends alone just to keep herself available for him. She had settled for living alone without the benefit of a girlfriend being a roommate for the convenience and privacy of having a married lover. She had settled for having male acquaintances to keep up a false appearance that she was dating and going out. She had settled to look the other way and throw caution to the wind for the love of a man that was not hers. She had settled to live a life of secrecy, deception, and adultery. Bottom line, she had settled for being the other woman.

Wednesday nights were usually her worst times with Edgar. The guilt and shame would weigh heavily upon her conscience after attending mid-week service. By the time he would ease into her bed on Wednesday nights her tears, begging, and pleading for him to get a divorce had become normal. Edgar had perfected his art of reassuring and settling her mind that their love was worth the wait. Before the night was over, she would be right back where she started—madly in love with a man that was married to someone else. A man whom she couldn't call her very own.

The weekend finally arrived. Edgar cleared his Saturday night and promised Serena that she could have him for the rest of the weekend, including all day on Sunday. He gave his familiar tap on the door before using his key. Instead of the anticipated hugging and kissing, it was apparent that Serena was in a somber mood.

"Look baby, this is Saturday," he laughed. "It's the golden time of the day when you kick back and relax with the one you love. I don't have time for all this soul searching crap. For a minute, I thought it was Wednesday night, and we know how hard I have to work to get you in the mood."

He joined her on the couch and pulled her close to him. Gently, he pressed soft kisses along her neckline.

"Come on babycakes, I'm in no mood for an interrogation," he whispered softly in her ear. "We know how this scene is going to play out. So, let's just cut the chase and enjoy each other's company. You're wasting valuable time."

Serena didn't answer. Instead, she got up from the couch and went to the small closet in the living room. She had packed his things. With an oversized gym bag in her hand, she held it out for his reach. Edgar's stunned but amused smile only infuriated her. Whenever she wanted to discuss their future together, he found clever words and expressions to distract her and make light of their situation. She could feel her anger, hurt, disappointment, and remorse for being in a relationship with him brewing up like a festering boil that was about to burst.

But, this time, it was going to be different. She would not let her emotions take control and give into the crying, and an emotional upheaval that always ended with her tears of apologies, and his broken promises of commitment. Addicted like a junkie, and without thought of moral or spiritual consciousness, she would give her body to him completely as though they were one in marriage, body, and mind. But today, something deep inside of her spirit had spoken to her soul.

Serena looked at the distinguished looking man she had wanted to call her own at any cost. The man she had given her heart, body, and soul to for the past four years. She closed her eyes and took a deep sigh to find the strength to do what needed to be done.

"Edgar, I've had enough," she stated calmly with the gym bag still extended towards him. "These are all of your things including your rum, gin, cognac, and personal toiletry items. You can keep the key because I'll be moving out. And, since you've seen to paying my rent up for the next few months, you can have the apartment. Just make sure you put your name on the lease."

Edgar could hardly believe his ears. Within the last year, she had had her emotional scenes, but she had never gone this far. Maybe, he should play this little scene out with her. He was certain that she wasn't strong enough to leave him and he wasn't about to let her go. They were a long way from being over in his mind.

"Oh, you've had enough," his eyes were laughing with disbelief. "And by giving me my things and moving out, you think we will be finished? Look baby, we're talking about love here. You loving me and me loving you. Let me see you walk away from that truth."

No tears came because she had cried out of tears. No long soul wrenching discussion would happen because she had talked out. There would be no pleading and begging because her heart was numb. The truth and reality was that she had had enough.

"Yes, I love you Edgar, but it's not the right kind of love. It's not the love that God would have for us. You're married and belong to someone else. I need and want a husband to call my own. It's just that simple."

Edgar kept his amused expression but for some reason he detected a different state of calmness in her. "Look baby, you've gotten yourself worked up. You're letting all this church going, and Bible reading, mess up your lifestyle. You're young and beautiful. At your age life allows you to live, love, and laugh."

Serena moved closer to the front door. Again, she looked long and hard at this man she had loved unconditionally for the past four years. She could see the uncertainty slowing creeping into his eyes. She continued from somewhere deep inside of her soul.

"Edgar, please let me go. I can't go on like this. I can't continue to live like this. I'm dying on the inside. Every day, I lose a little bit more of myself. You can help me by letting me go. Please, if you truly love me then let me go."

Edgar was not prepared for such a sincere outcry. She was any man's dream for a friend, wife, and lover. Selfishly, he had held onto her. He should've released her long ago, but the truth of the matter was that he couldn't. She was really stronger than him.

His voice sounded low and raspy. "You're serious, aren't you? Just like that you expect me to leave and walk away. Serena, I never lied to you. I've always been up front and honest about my situation. You knew the odds here. I know things haven't worked out just as I expected but it's getting there. The divorce is just a matter of time. She's going to let me go soon because she knows my heart isn't with her. Look baby, we've come this far, just hold on a little while longer. Soon, I promise, we'll be together."

Serena could hear the pleading in his voice but it didn't move her this time. This time was the last time. If she had one more conversation about their future, she felt like she would die.

"Please Edgar, I'm not changing my mind. I've had enough...it's over....we're over. Please....leave....just leave."

Hurt and angry, but most of all shocked, Edgar snatched up the gym bag and walked out the door. He turned on the walkway and gave her one last look.

"It's not going to be easy you know. I'll give you time to reconsider. Take a few days to really think about our future together and what you're throwing away. I'll wait on your call because you will be calling."

Serena watched as he pulled off into the sunset and until his car disappeared. She walked onto her small balcony porch and sat on one of the wicker lounge seats. It was a beautiful, peaceful, summer night, and the breeze was warm and refreshing. She drew her shapely legs up to her chest and hugged them close to her heart. Looking upward into the darkening sky, she smiled and communed with a heavenly spirit, which she hadn't visited in some time.

"Oh Edgar, you're so very wrong," she sighed heavily. "Today, I gave my life back to my higher power. I've never given this burden over to the Lord like this before. And, he has promised to never forsake me or leave me alone. No temptation has seized me, but that which is common to man, and if I'm faithful, God will give me a way out so that I can stand. So Edgar, my prayer is that you will find the peace that I've found. But, my sincerest prayer, is that the Lord will give me a husband that I can call my own."

Serena closed her eyes and let the stillness of the night minister to her in a way that only a higher and heavenly power could do.

It was four o'clock, on a Sunday morning, and Cecil Isaac "Ike" Webb couldn't sleep. Six months ago, and prior to his relocation to Memphis, he would just be coming in from his Saturday night partying.

Ike got out of bed and walked around in his new condo. Everything that was going on in his life was confirmation of a new beginning.

At thirty years of age, and for the first time in his life, he had never felt so satisfied and content. He thought about how far he had come and some of the wild and crazy things that he had done and survived. "If walls could talk and if the story could be told," he laughed loudly. "I should be a dead man six feet under."

Even though he was content with his new manager's job at FedEx, there was still something missing from his life that he couldn't explain. It seemed the harder he worked, and the more he accomplished, the bigger the ache and void became.

"This must be a sign of how it feels to need Jesus in your life," he thought. "Maybe, I need to find the Lord."

He grabbed the remote control and surfed channels. He stopped surfing and listened to the man preaching about what a wonderful change that had come over his life. "Yeah, I need Jesus," he stated loudly.

Ike managed a team of twelve couriers. But, there were a lot of days when he was back in the truck making deliveries himself. Some nights all he could do was fall in bed, and sleep like a baby until his four o'clock alarm woke him up to start all over again. He loved it! He was the happiest new manager at the company.

Three nights a week he went to the gym. His six feet, muscular, broad shoulder frame, was toned and fit. He wore his hair cut close and was only a decision away from shaving it bald. The summer heat had tanned him to a creamy shade of mocha brown. When he looked in the mirror, the image staring back resembled his deceased alcoholic father. But, he was known as Foxy Fox's boy, his playa's name and fame with the women.

"Foxy Fox" was Ike's mother, and her name was Clarice Webb. Ike had inherited her good looks. Clarice had done the best she could on a waitress salary raising Ike and his sister, Marlene, in Birmingham, Alabama. Ike knew his father, and how to find him at the local café, but he had never bonded with him. It wasn't until he was an adult that he went to visit his father in the hospital. As fate would have it, his father passed a few months later to alcohol abuse.

Clarice didn't attend church or raise her children up in the church. Their churching depended upon local churches that would come and gather up children for outreach events. It was only when Ike and Marlene would go to their grandmother's house in St. Louis that any Christian teaching would be given to them.

Ike's teenage years were spent unsupervised. It was a known fact that he didn't have to go far from home for a party. A party was always going on at Clarice's house with her on and off again lovers. Ike would do just enough to come within an inch from being with the wrong crowd or going to jail. The way he figured it, and the way Clarice had raised him, if he wanted to smoke weed or drink, he could do that at home. Why go to jail, when he could have any girl or woman he desired.

He didn't want any babies either. Clarice had taught them everything they wanted to know and didn't want to know about sex and birth control. When his sister, Marlene got pregnant and eloped, Clarice was upset and broken-hearted.

"I don't know why she got married. I didn't bring her up like that. Now she's in bondage and trapped in tradition," Clarice cried into her beer glass, talking loud, and to anyone who was drinking with her. Most of the time it was Ike or Marlene, sitting at her kitchen table, trying to persuade her to move and change her lifestyle.

"Y'all are my babies and I didn't do nothing but love y'all," she tuned up, needing to justify the way she raised them. "I know my lifestyle ain't proper, but I ain't never let no man hurt and abuse us. It ain't no harm in drinking a little beer, playing cards, and listening to good music, and that's what I like to do. I know y'all Granny says that my soul is going to hell, but that's because she don't know nothing about living. And, I ain't gone tolerate y'all bad mouthing me either. I love and respect y'all and I want the same respect. I'm about the most open minded mother you'll ever find. I'm teaching y'all about real life, this world, and how to survive."

There was so much Ike wanted to say to his mother. So many unexpressed feelings and emotions but he never knew how. He never knew how to tell her that he wished she'd done better by raising them. He wished she'd done better by giving him a male figure in his life. He wished she'd been focused on him and Marlene rather than her beauty and ability to get any man that she thought she wanted.

When it was time for him to relocate to his new job in Memphis all he could do was hug her. "Cecil Isaac Webb, I don't believe you're going to just up and leave us like this. Boy, me and Marlene is all you got. We need to stay a family right here in Birmingham. Why are you just telling me two days before you leave? I would've thrown you a going away party," Clarice stated, popping open a can of beer and smoking a cigarette.

"Mama, that's why I'm telling you now. Because I don't want a going away party. I've changed. I want something more out of life than just living here in Birmingham and partying on the weekends."

Deep down within, Clarice knew she had failed her children, and it always hurt deeply and brought her to tears.

Ike gave her a hug and kiss. "I'll be calling you Mama when I get settled. Marlene knows how to contact me if you need me," he said lovingly. "And, please lay off the beer and cigarettes. It's not good for your high blood pressure. I want you to be well. Mama, do it for me, would you please?"

"Go on boy," she cried. "You're still trying to take care of me. I want to see what you're doing with your life. Just don't be getting married. You too good looking and handsome for somebody to be talking about they got papers on you. I never did believe in that mess. Ain't nobody gone ever have papers on me and that's a fact Jack!"

Isaac left his mother's house with a heavy heart. He knew both of their lives were missing something. And, he wanted it for his mother just as bad as he wanted it for himself. He had never been a praying man but lately it seemed that it was all he had a mind to do.

"Lord, help my Mother and please help me. Whatever it is that we're missing and searching for in life help us find it."

Audra "Dimples" Carey, watched as Ike completed a check ride with one of the couriers. He was one of the hardest working managers she'd seen in the five years she'd worked at FedEx. Plus, he was single, good looking, and searching for something to fill a void in his life. She decided that she was just what he needed.

She had timed his arrival back to the station and had ordered salad and pizza. She waited on him in the breakroom knowing that he would welcome lunch. "Ike, I've being thinking about our conversation this morning," Dimples stated, motioning for him to join her. "I think the missing dimension in your life is spiritual."

The bagel and coffee he'd eaten at breakfast had digested and he was starving. Dimples made it a priority to fill in the blanks about his life and it kept him amused. Ike liked Dimples' carefree spirit. He had escorted her to a few social functions and she in turn had done the same for him. Dimples was safe and not looking for a committed relationship and that's exactly what he wanted.

"Dimples, how can you be so certain? You don't know enough about me. For all you know, I could be a preacher on the run from the church or something."

"Now, that would be even better," Dimples grinned. "Single, good looking, good job, saved, and a preacher. You're a girl's dream Rev. Ike."

Ike's eyes twinkled with amusement. His arm touched Dimples' hand as he reached over to get another slice of the meat lover's pizza.

"Rev. Ike, now that's the last person in the world I want to be identified with. I've gone from Don Juan to Rev. Ike. No wonder I'm feeling all tapped out."

Dimples could still feel the touch of Ike's arm brushing against her hand. She wished that the relationship between them could be of a different nature. She liked Ike from the very first day she'd set eyes on him. Part of her duties as a Customer Service Agent, was helping him get acclimated to his new duties and moving around in a new city. It didn't take long for her to assess that Ike had been a partier and womanizer. She was certain that this job and relocation was a fresh start on a new life.

"Well Ike, if it's not spiritual, then it's that little matter of age and settling down. Are you familiar with the word marriage? For some reason marriage, wife, and children have escaped you. How is that?" she inquired.

Ike swallowed his last bite of pizza and gathered his dispatch radio and clipboard. "Exactly, I'm not the marrying kind," he responded with a mouthful of pizza. "You've just demonstrated the surest and quickest way to get rid of me by mentioning that subject. You were doing better staying on the church topic."

"Coward, coward, coward," Dimples shouted to Ike's backside as he made a quick exit from the breakroom. "I'll be looking for you at Wednesday night church service. And, if you don't show up, I'll keep bringing up that four letter word marriage every day for the next six months."

On Wednesday night, instead of going to the gym, Ike sat in his parked car across the street from the Faith Baptist Church. He watched the people enter for mid-week service. For three weeks, he had parked and watched the people. He would drive off and leave empty, lost, lonely, and confused.

On this night, he finally got out of the car, and went inside. The sound of praise and worship filled the corridor as he waited to enter. He liked the feel of the small church. Faith Baptist reminded him of his grandmother's church. When the doors opened, he was greeted with a warm, sweet spirit, and immediately felt welcomed.

He took a seat on one of the back pews and took in the atmosphere of the on-fire spirit-filled prayers being prayed. He spotted Dimples in the choir stand with her eyes closed and hands lifted up. She hadn't seen him enter and he doubted if he would stay until the end of the service. This was good because he wouldn't feel obligated to stay to the end of service.

What he wasn't prepared for was the vision of loveliness that caught his eye on the first row in the choir stand. She was sitting three persons down from Dimples. For a brief second, he felt as if his heart had stopped beating. All kind of thoughts were going through his mind.

"How could this be? I haven't been in this church five minutes and already I'm on the prowl. Will I ever change? Maybe, I do have a sickness or something," he pondered within himself. He resolved that he truly needed God's help. He bowed his head in shame and prayed silently.

"Lord, help me make a change. I want more out of life than just chasing skirts. Teach me how to appreciate a woman for other than carnal reasons. Lord, I'm in need of something meaningful in my life that will fulfill this emptiness and loneliness. Lord, show me what I need. Help me Lord."

Ike knew with certainty that he wanted to become a part of this church. He didn't hesitate to get up from his seat, and proceed down the aisle, when Pastor Kenton opened the doors to the church. He wasn't sure what to do when Mack Earl jumped up and ran down the aisle ahead of him. But, Pastor Kenton's warm smile, and nod of approval encourage Ike to come forward. The shouting and praising was overwhelming on this Wednesday night.

Dimples wanted to run up and down the aisles. She couldn't explain the joy and pride she felt watching Ike accept the invitation to Christian discipleship.

"That's him, that's him," she whispered to everyone in ear shot. "That's my friend and coworker. He finally came and he joined."

Before she knew it she had eased down the row and stood next to Serena. "Oh, I'm so happy, happy, happy," Dimples, spoke softly.

"You had no idea he was coming tonight," Serena whispered back, while Pastor Kenton continued the appeal to the nearly full congregation.

"None whatsoever," Dimples responded, trying to contain her excitement. "Serena, I'm crazy about him. I got this feeling that he's the one for me. Oh God, I pray that he's the one for me."

Serena gave her best friend a hug. "If it's meant to be it will be. Just put it in God's hands. He knows our needs."

Ike publicly professed a hope in Christ. He accepted the ordinance of baptism for the upcoming Sunday service. He was assigned a new member's deacon, Samuel Garrett. Pastor Kenton acknowledged Dimples for leading a new member to the Lord and to their church family.

Immediately after the service, Ike's new
church family rushed to shake his hand and
welcome him to Faith Baptist. Dimples gave
him a warm embrace and proceeded to
introduce him to each member. By the time Serena came
from the choir room she was the last person in the line.

"Hello, my name is Serena Garrett and welcome to
Faith Baptist," she smiled, extending her hand to Ike.
"Dimples says nothing but good things about you. We're so
very glad to have you here."

"It's good to be here," Ike responded back, making a
mental note of the woman's name that had captured his
heart at first glance.

Dimples held onto Ike's free hand with a big smile on
her face. "Ike, Serena is my best girlfriend in the world.
We're all in the same circle now and this is a good night to
celebrate. Usually, a few of us eat out on Wednesday nights,
and you'll just have to come with us. Serena, can't you give
us one hour beyond your self-imposed curfew?"

"I have to decline," Serena stated.

"I'm sorry, same here," Ike declined regretfully.

He gave Dimples a hug and thanked her for inviting
him. He knew they would have a lot to talk about. Dimples
would tell him everything that he needed to know and
everything that he didn't want to know.

Returning to his car, he knew he had made the right
decision. Faith Baptist was something positive and he
needed some new inspiration. Just as he turned his
headlights on he caught a glimpse of Serena's profile driving
off in a black Mercedes. There it was again the feeling that
went straight to his heart.

How could he feel this way about someone he had
just met? He didn't know if she was married or single, but
he knew that he had to put his feelings in check. This was
the very thing that he was fighting. Satan wouldn't catch

him in the same old trap anymore. He was in church, with a new church family, and his mind would be focused on those things that were righteous and pleasing to God.

Ike prayed as he moved into the departing traffic while following closely behind the black Mercedes. *"Lord, thank you for this new beginning. Keep my heart pure and my mind stayed on you."*

 On Sunday, Ike was totally focused on Pastor Kenton's sermon. He had never felt so inspired from the preached word. Neither, did he imagine that he would be filled with such a tremendous sense of peace during his baptism.

Ike was overjoyed when he looked out in the audience and saw Clarice and Marlene. His heart was broken when he'd called the night before. Clarice was making excuses for not coming, but Marlene had promised to bring her if she had to knock her unconscious. Just before the benediction, Pastor Kenton asked Ike to say a few words to his new church family. Ike felt nervous in this new setting but he stood before the church and spoke from his heart.

"When I was twelve, I was supposed to have gotten baptized at a church in my neighborhood. But, a few of us decided it wasn't important. So we sneaked out the church and went to play basketball. After that I just told people that I had been baptized so nobody would worry me about it again. Today, I can say that I stayed and got baptized."

He glanced over at his mother and sister and smiled. He could see Dimples wiping tears of joy. His assigned deacon, Samuel Garrett, was sitting on the front bench, and nodding with approval at Ike's open testimony. Ike felt a sense of comfort and security. Sensing the warmth and friendliness coming from the audience, he continued to speak.

"I'm just glad that the Lord didn't have to knock me down to get my attention. For so long my life has been incomplete. I felt like I didn't have a purpose in life. I tried to fill it with a lot of worldly things, but still something was missing. Now, I know what was missing, and I've come alive. I thank God that Satan didn't get my mind. Somebody out there must've been praying for me. I've got a lot of spiritual growing to do, and all I can say is that I'm ready to be a new man."

Ike took his seat and openly wiped his tears as they trickled down his face. He didn't care who saw him and what they would think about his newly found peace. He was just simply thankful to have found it himself.

From the choir stand, Serena admired his honesty and sincere remarks. She could feel her own tears flowing. She wasn't crying for his happiness, but for her own sense of incompleteness and lost joy.

She bowed her head on her own behalf. *"Oh, Lord, help me. Give me a fresh start and new love. My heart is heavy, my life is empty, and incomplete. I've let sin abide and take over. Lord, please grant unto me your restoration and peace."*

 "Come in and make yourselves at home," Sam instructed Ike, Clarice, and Marlene. "I'm this young man's deacon and he's under my watch and that means so is his people. Ain't nobody eating at any restaurants today. We're going to enjoy getting to know each other."

Sam and Gladys had invited a small group over to celebrate Ike's baptism. Their brick, three bedroom, two full baths home was immaculate and comfortable. Sam took great pride in the recent addition of the large family room on the back of the house. He had laid every brick himself as he would announce when showing off the new room.

Sam had become quite the housekeeper since Gladys' rheumatoid arthritis had made her semi-dependent on a mobility walker. He started off with her supervision on dusting and washing. She did all the cooking and still maintained her vegetable and flower gardens. Sam did the digging and planting and she would do the watering, pruning, singing, and nurturing of the garden. Her gardens were her sanctuary and place to commune with God.

As Gladys' arthritis became more debilitating, she upgraded to a Hoveround power chair. Sam went out of his way to build accessible front and back ramps for her mobility. She became quite efficient in maneuvering to do just about anything she set her mind on. Especially, driving herself across the street to the church. She was determined to overcome her mobility challenges.

Serena showed Clarice and Marlene to the guest room for them to change and freshen up. Ike waited his turn and she led him to the room she had occupied as a child.

"Just make yourself as comfortable as you can," she laughed, emptying a chair full of stuffed animals and tossing them onto the bed. "I hope you can stomach all of this pink and lavendar for a few minutes."

Ike's amusement showed on his face. "You must have been one spoiled kid," he teased. "Did you ask for every doll on the market?"

"Practically," Serena grinned, as she averted her attention to the twenty or more dolls aligned on the shelved wall. "Mother says that she is saving them for my daughters, but she's the collector. I think she enjoyed shopping for dolls and I was just the excuse."

Ike admired the colorful bedroom that depicted a girl's childhood, teenage, and early college years.

"It must have been nice to have this much love growing up," he stated. "You're blessed Serena, and you should never take that for granted."

Serena detected a hint of sadness in his voice. "Yes, there was a time that I did take it for granted, but now I know better. And, if the Lord ever blesses me with children of my own, I'll probably be to them just like my parents are about me. And, my children, will probably be about me, just like I was to my parents, foolish and rebellious."

Ike laughed at her expressions and the light heartedness of her mood. She appeared relaxed and comfortable. He felt a little nervous and apprehensive because it seemed if he was developing some real feelings for her. Again, that familiar feeling of wanting to know her sexually was creeping into his thoughts. He had to change his thinking and get his mind off his carnal desires.

For the past six months, he had been so consumed with his new job, settling into a new city, and asking God for a new way of life, until living an abstinent lifestyle hadn't been a problem. It was a welcomed relief. It wasn't until he met Serena that these feelings were being awakened.

For a brief second their eyes met and something passed between them. They both heard the laughter of Dimples and other church members arriving in the living room. Ike quickly averted his attention beyond the open door and into the hallway. Serena's heart seemed to have skipped a beat from the unexpected impact of looking into his romantic eyes. She had taken his look towards the open door as an indication that he was glad Dimples had arrived.

"I'm just talking and you need to change," she mumbled, walking out into the hall. "It sounds like Dimples is here and I'm sure my help is needed in the kitchen."

"Yes, I need to change," Ike's response sounded a bit nervous as well. "Tell Dimples that I will be out soon."

"I sure will," Serena smiled, closing the bedroom door behind her.

Seeing that no one was utilizing the guest bathroom, she escaped for a few minutes to be alone with her thoughts.

"Hold up a minute honey child," her image whispered back to her from the mirror. "I know you ain't trying to have no feelings for this man. Is your hormones tripping or what? You haven't gotten out of the mess that you're already in. What makes you think that man will ever be interested in you? You are damaged goods and don't you ever forget it."

Serena dropped her head and felt the all too familiar feeling of guilt and shame. Quickly, she patted some cold water on her cheeks and fussed over her hair a few minutes longer. "At least you can act like you're happy," she told herself. She flashed a forced smile and put on her happiest face to greet her parent's guests. She promised herself that she would have a decent Sunday evening for a change.

Ike quickly changed into a pair of khaki pants and a pullover shirt. He discarded his dress socks and kept on his black, soft leather, Italian loafers. He stared at his image from the mirror and frowned. Staring back at him was a pretty boy, GQ player's image. It was an image that he had grown to dislike because of the many women and affairs that he'd been involved. He was ashamed of his past and how he had exploited himself and the women that he had taken up with.

How could God use somebody like him? How could he ever wish or hope to have a decent, saved, educated, successful, and beautiful church going woman like Serena? He definitely had to keep his eyes focused on God.

*"Help me Lord. You know my heart and my heart desires.
Keep my mind focused on you and spiritual things."*

Ike was glad that Dimples had been invited. She
would help distract his mind from Serena. Sooner or later he
was going to have to tell someone about his feelings for
Serena, and Dimples was his best confidant. He headed to
the living room to enjoy an evening of food, fun, and
fellowship with his new church family.

Gladys had orchestrated quite a feast for Ike's
baptismal dinner. Tender grilled filet mignon
steaks, fried chicken, potato salad, three bean
salad, fruit salads, and fresh turnip greens from her garden.
Pastor Kenton and First Lady Marie Kenton brought a three-
layered, triple chocolate, devil's food cake that was the talk
of the dessert table. The Mission Circle women had provided
homemade ice cream for the dinner celebration.

Dimples added to the spread by bringing her melt-in-
your-mouth award winning peach cobbler. After the
blessing, everyone served themselves buffet style and ate
heartily. When the desserts and homemade ice cream were
set out, everyone was getting second and third servings.
The conversations were loud and chatty and everybody had
something to talk about.

"Isaac needs to be pistol-whipped," Clarice stated to
Pastor Kenton. "I didn't know that he hadn't been baptized.
I sent him to that church to get baptized. He's fooled us all
these years."

Marlene quickly gave her mother one of her irritated
looks. "Mama, he's baptized now and that's the important
thing. Let's just thank God that he has a church family now."

"It's just the truth," Clarice voice came across a little shaken. "I may not have taken y'all to church, but I got enough spirituality to know that you at least need to be baptized. Pastor Kenton, if I had known he wasn't baptized I would have called those people to come back and get him."

Ike overheard enough of the conversation to know that he would need to keep Clarice and Marlene tempers in check. The last thing he wanted was for Clarice to go into a song and dance about their upbringing, and what she couldn't and didn't do for them as a single parent. One subject that she and Marlene definitely bumped heads on was their upbringing and this was not the time or place.

"That's right Mama, I was quite mischievous," Ike stated, while pulling up a chair next to Clarice. "Aren't you glad that I admitted it and did something about it?"

"Isaac, your grandmother would've gotten off her sick bed and snatched me up if she had known that before she passed. God rest her soul."

Ike's charm always melted Clarice no matter what he had done. She could see in his eyes that he wanted her and Marlene on their best behavior. She was a sucker for him because he was a combination of her and his father's good looks. Together they had created a handsome son. It was obvious that in her younger years she was definitely a Foxy Fox. Even now, at age fifty-three, she was still an attractive woman, but the signs of heavy cigarette smoking, beer drinking, and worldly living were wearing on her.

"Come on and give your Mama a hug. I just never thought my boy would end up in the church. Between you and Marlene I ain't got a chance. I'm going to have to clean up my act sooner or later. Say a prayer for me whiles you sending up them prayers," she sighed.

Ike hugged his mother close and with a soft voice he appealed to her. "Mama, every day I say a prayer for you that you would just open up your heart, forgive yourself, and let God love you. Mama, salvation is a free gift. All you have to do is want it," Ike pleaded softly.

Pastor Kenton and the others who were sitting around the dining room table listened as Ike caringly and lovingly talked to his mother. It was apparent that he wanted her to give her life to Christ.

Pastor Kenton left his seat and came to stand beside Clarice and Ike. "I would like for everyone to stop what you're doing. It's prayer time. God is doing something here. We must recognize it and let him have his way."

Pastor Kenton stood behind Clarice and placed both of his hands on her shoulders. A fervent prayer was prayed on behalf of Clarice Webb. Marlene came and knelt beside her Mother and held onto her and Isaac's hand. Like Isaac, she wanted with her whole heart that their mother would change her lifestyle. There wasn't a dry eye in the house when the prayer had ended.

"I'm sorry," Clarice cried tearfully. "I didn't mean to come here and embarrass my son in his new life and with his new friends. I should have just stayed in Birmingham."

Serena was overtaken with the touching scene. She went to Clarice's side to reassure her. "Oh no, Mrs. Webb," she smiled through her own misty eyes. "You belong here. You're in the right place today. I believe God wanted this to happen just the way it happened. You don't have to apologize for anything. We love you just the way you are."

Clarice squeezed Serena's hand and gave her a wink. "Thank you. Everyone is so kind and nice. I've never met such a nice group of people, and especially you. Ike talks about you all the time when he calls home."

Serena quickly corrected her. "Mrs. Webb, I've just met Ike on Wednesday night," Serena stated. "You must be referring to Dimples."

Clarice corrected her error. "Oh, I'm sorry...it's Dimples who works with him. He says such nice things about all of y'all. Do you mind if I step outside and smoke a cigarette?"

"Of course not, Mrs. Webb," Serena stammered. "I'll take you out on the patio where its comfortable."

Ike watched as Clarice and Serena left the room. He was tempted to go outside with them, but Dimples had everyone's attention with her stories of his first days on the job. He was amused but his thoughts drifted to Serena. He was constantly glancing in her direction. Her natural beauty, charming style, and laughter captivated him. The soft lavender, tee-strapped, two-piece Capri pant outfit that she was wearing complimented her warm brown skin, and shapely round figure. He kept noticing her pretty legs, and the gentle movement of her hips. She was a little shorter than the women he was usually attracted to, but he could tell she would be a perfect fit in his arms. She was quite the hostess and very receptive to his mother and sister's comfort and that he liked.

"Mrs. Webb, I've been instructed to prepare the extra bedroom for you and Marlene," Serena stated under the well-shaded covered patio. "It's going to be too late for the two of you to drive back  tonight. Plus, my father and Ike have already made the decision and Marlene agreed."

"Thank you Lord," Clarice laughed, putting out her cigarette, and sitting next to Serena on the porch swing. "I was dreading that ride back. I wouldn't have been worth two dead flies trying to keep Marlene awake."

Serena's delightful laugh filled the air. "Ike said that you wouldn't mind. Plus, he said that you would rather stay here then go back to his place because you wouldn't have wanted to sleep on the let out sofa."

Clarice looked surprised but laughed also. "That boy sure does know his Mama. I didn't mind about the sofa. It was getting up at four o'clock in the morning and getting on the road that early. Staying over here, Marlene would never wake up somebody's household that early."

"Well good, I'm glad you're staying overnight. It will make my parents happy. Don't worry, my father has already said that he wasn't getting anybody up and out until they had a good night's sleep. He'll have y'all on the road after breakfast and at a decent hour."

Clarice lit up another cigarette and doused it out before she even put it up to her mouth. She didn't like pretending to be something she wasn't, and she wasn't going to feel right until she clarified her marital status with Serena.

"Serena, I'm very easy to get along with," she blurted out. "I ain't never been married, and I don't try to pretend that I ever have been. I had two children by two different men, and I don't apologize for it. And furthermore, call me Clarice. I would prefer that and we'll get along just fine."

Again, Serena was a little startled by Clarice's directness. "I'm sorry. I didn't mean to offend you. I can call you Clarice...," Serena stammered.

"Good!" Clarice smiled and gave her a pat on her hand. "See you and me are off to a good start already."

Serena and Clarice sat quietly side by side on the patio swing listening to the loud laughter coming from the house. Clarice was comfortable with Serena and Serena was comfortable with Clarice.

"I hope I'm not all out of my tree if I said something," Clarice looked at Serena curiously. "But, I feel like I can speak openly with you."

Once again, Serena's expression indicated her surprise, but she was curious. "Yes ma'am....Clarice. Please say what's on your mind."

Clarice took her time before speaking. "Serena, I want you to know this before I leave here. Now, I did confuse you with Dimples, but Isaac doesn't look at Dimples the way he looks at you. I've been noticing how my son has been watching you this evening. He'll tell you that I'm not one who takes marriage very seriously because a piece of paper don't say you own a man. But, I just got this feeling that Ike is looking for a wife, and he probably needs a wife. Now, if I ever have to give my acceptance to my son getting married, it would be for you. Yes ma'am, my baby, Foxy's boy, has made a big change. I never thought I'd want to see this day, but it's here, and I can live with it. My son needs a wife."

For the first time in a long time, Serena was speechless. It took her a few minutes but she found her voice. "Clarice, I don't know," Serena gasped. "All of this is too soon to even comment on. Dimples and Ike seem to be getting along just fine. Plus, I'm involved and coming out of a bad relationship right now. I just don't see it."

"Well I feel it," Clarice said knowingly. "I can't believe I'm quoting my good ol' dead Mama, may God rest her soul, but we'll just have to see what the good Lord has to say about all of this. And, whoever you seemed to be anguishing about, ain't got a chance, if my Ike got his heart set on you. Something tells me some stuff is going to be stirred up. What's done in the dark is coming to the light."

Serena was beyond speechless. She and Clarice fell into a comfortable silence and enjoyed the evening air, while watching the sun set behind the western skyline. They both wondered about the future and just how both their lives and future happiness would all turn out.

"Only time will tell," Serena sighed.

"You got that right," Clarice sighed heavily.

Friday's early morning air smelled of rain. Serena was praying that the rain wouldn't come until the movers had unloaded her furniture. She was moving back to her parent's house.

Three weeks had passed since she'd ended the affair with Edgar. She would be the first to admit that every morning she started her day with a heavy heart. At work, it had been hard seeing him coming and going without any interaction between them. His attitude had been cheerful with others but distant with her. She knew he was hiding behind an arrogant façade, which was his way for punishing her for ending the relationship.

Twice in one week she had called his desk telephone, but quickly hung up before he could answer. A couple of times she had answered her telephone at home with no response from the person on the other end. No doubt that it was Edgar calling from his home. She had been tempted to speak but something deep within her just couldn't do it any longer. After a few minutes of silence, she would gently place the receiver back into its holder.

Her nights were teary and unbearable and she would always end up on her knees crying out for God's help. After thoroughly weighing all of her options, she made the decision to quit her job to attend graduate school, and follow her dream of becoming a counselor.

Sam and Gladys were thrilled that Serena was moving back home. Gladys felt in her heart that Serena had been carrying a heavy burden for some time. It was not her style to pry into Serena's business. She only wanted to be a listening ear and a guiding voice. Gladys listened with her heart and a mother's ear at Serena's explanation for why she was moving back home.

"Mom, I need to change some things in my life," Serena said somberly. "I've decided to go to school full time in the fall and get a master's degree. I'll apply for financial aid, but rent and utilities will be quite a lot without a job. Plus, I've paid enough rent and it's time I think about investing in some real estate of my own."

"Now you're talking with some sense," Sam chuckled. "Get you some equity. Baby girl, this is home and the door is always open. Now, I got to go meet up with my fishing buddy."

"Thanks Daddy," Serena smiled. "I was kind of expecting a lecture or something on the prodigal daughter returning home."

Sam turned his gaze to Serena and smiled. "You came back right young lady. You've done nothing but made us proud. I only got one expectation of you," he said sternly.

Serena and Gladys both looked at each curiously and awaited his next words. The corners of his mouth curved into a smile. "You are going to have to learn how to cook if you're coming back up in this camp," Sam grinned. "You can learn everything else. Picking greens and cleaning fish is a requirement in this house."

"Samuel Garrett," Gladys scowled. "You need to get on out that door. Ain't nobody cleaning any stinking fish. You don't do nothing but give it away to everybody in the neighborhood."

"That's my point," he grinned. "Serena can clean it, cook it, and then we can sell fish sandwiches. I always did want to open me a little sandwich store."

Serena moved close to her father and ran her fingers lovingly through his thinning soft gray hair. "No problem, Dad," she kissed his cheek. "I'll pick the greens but you're on your own with the fish."

"I love you baby girl," Sam kissed her back. "What's ours is yours. Welcome home!"

Serena watched as her father walked across the street to the church and got in the car with Pastor Kenton. She was happy that he was still in such good health for his age. He was so full of life and adventure. She'd been born to them late in their marriage and they felt especially blessed by having her, and she felt blessed to have them as parents. She felt fortunate to have a father that loved and cared for her mother with so much love. He'd given her a wonderful example of a husband and father's love.

Serena could feel Gladys watchful eyes studying her from across the room. She stared at her father's old armchair, which was worn and needed new upholstery. Since being home, she saw the little things that were going undone. Why hadn't she seen earlier that she was needed at home? Sam was doing a good job with the housecleaning, but it missed Gladys' decorative touch. Everything was in order, but it was all so old and dated.

"Well Mom, you thought you would never see this day," Serena sighed, flopping down in the chair across from her mother.

Gladys pulled her basket onto her lap and started matching quilting squares. She looked up at Serena and smiled. "And what a good day it is," she stated lovingly. "I'm just thankful you know that home is a good place to come for refuge and healing."

Serena could feel the hot burning tears welling up in her eyes and just waiting to spill out. But how could she tell her mother the awful state of her heart and the sinful life she had been living. How would her mother ever understand? Was it necessary for her to confess her sins to her mother? Is this what God wanted her to do?

"Oh Mama," Serena sighed heavily. "I've made some terrible decisions in the last seven years. I've done things that I'm not proud of and I don't think I'll ever want to tell them to anyone as long as I live."

"I know you know who you can tell," Gladys eyes smiled. "If we confess our sins God is faithful and just and he will forgive us of all unrighteousness. Serena, you know God's word. Use it as a lamp unto your feet. Sweetheart, draw near to him and he'll see you through."

"Yes Mama. I know that now. I hadn't wanted to let go and let God but it's too big for me and I need his help. Mama, I'm coming back home with a broken heart and a broken spirit. All I can do is to pray, and just try to put one foot in front of the other, one day at a time. I got myself into this mess and I don't know what else to do."

"You're doing what's right and that's the important thing. Confess your sins to the Lord, believe that he has forgiven you, and turn away from that which separates you from his love. That's the only way to be fully restored. And when God fixes it, it's fixed. I just believe in my heart that the fix is in place and the way has been made for whatever has befallen you."

Serena moved into her mother's arms and her tears flowed freely. She cried for her lonely and wasted years. She cried for repentance. She cried to be taken back to a time in her life when she first believed, and had loved the Lord with her whole being. She cried for having the love of aging parents who had loved her completely. Finally, she cried for the joy and peace that was suddenly beginning to fill the brokenness in her heart.

"Thank you Lord, thank you Lord," Gladys whispered softly, while stroking Serena's bowed and tear-stricken face. "Serena, all is well. It is well with your soul. Rest my child…just rest in the Lord."

Later that night, Serena adjusted to being in the guest room. Both she and Gladys had thought it best to keep her bedroom just the way it was for sentimental reasons. The guest room was a little more spacious and provided a wonderful view of Gladys' flower garden.

Spreading cold cream all over her face, Serena admired the homey décor of her new bedroom. She had put her touch to the room with bright new colorful accessories. Not wanting any reminders of her past, especially her bedroom, she put all of her furniture in storage. She was willing to give it all away to the first needy couple that came along.

She entered the hall bathroom to continue her nightly moisturizing. A smile came over her face remembering her father's response to giving up his bathroom.

"Shucks, we're not having many overnight guests these days," he chuckled, while clearing the extra bathroom for Serena. "I'll just take my beauty products back into our bathroom and you can have the run of this one. Maybe, that will be my next project. I can add on a bathroom for the grandchildren."

Serena reached into the linen closet and pulled out one of her fluffy hand towels. Already the small closet was running over with her towels and toiletries, but she wasn't complaining. She moved the telephone from the hallway into her bedroom. She decided against transferring her home telephone services. If this was going to be a clean break from Edgar, she had to cut all strings and conveniences. Too many conveniences had been their downfall. She always made it easy and comfortable for them to abide in their sinful lifestyles.

She returned to her bedroom and anxiously slipped between sheets that smelled of a fresh tropical scent. She laid quietly and stared at the clock flashing *9:30*. She wished that her life wasn't so lonely on a Friday night. Tears suddenly stung her eyes. She wished she could have brought herself to tell her mother the real truth behind her move. Would she ever tell anyone the dark secrets of her heart?

"Stop thinking about it," she scolded herself quietly. "How long will I feel this emptiness? Will my heart ever heal? Will it take me four years or longer to come out of this darkness? Will I ever find someone who loves me as much as I loved him?"

All kind of questions were running through her mind. She felt devastated. Slipping from under the covers, and onto the floor on bended knees, she bowed in prayer. Unable to speak or say a word, she sobbed hopelessly into her pillow.

"Oh Lord, what will my tomorrows bring?"

Bright sunlight flooded the bedroom. The sound of a lawnmower and men talking awakened her. It was Saturday morning and the clock was flashing *9:00*. Serena jumped out of bed while still half asleep. She looked out the window and saw Sam talking to a neighbor. She took in the scenery. The flower garden was a refreshing view to start anyone's day. Down the street, she could see other neighbors out working in their yards.

Most of the families knew one another by name and had looked out for each other's homes for years. Most of her friends had moved out of state, but their parents were still in the community. They would return home for holidays and special occasions with their families and children. Sam and Gladys would be the first on their lists to visit with their family stories and photographs.

Serena continued to take in the scenery when she noticed a parked car a few yards from her parent's home. It was Edgar. She was certain it was Edgar but a closer look would confirm it. There was no mistake about it because she could recognize an unmarked police car anywhere. Hurriedly, she turned from the window, pulled on a pair of cutoff jeans, and a tee-shirt. She slipped into a pair of tennis shoes. How long had he been watching her parent's house? What was he going to do? What was she going to do?

Just as she entered the hallway, the smell of bacon and fresh brewed coffee drew her towards the kitchen. She decided to go out from the back and come up from the side of the house so that she could get a good look at the car. Contemplating her course of action, she walked into the kitchen consumed in her thoughts. She was taken by surprise when she saw Ike at the stove cooking.

"Good morning Serena," Ike smiled cheerfully. "I was hoping the smell of breakfast would wake you."

"Ike," she said loudly. "What are you doing here? Where is my mother?"

Ike flipped an over-sized omelet onto a plate and added a twig of parsley and fresh cut tomatoes on the side. Just about that time, two crisp, lightly brown, pieces of bread popped out the toaster.

"Would you prefer jam or honey with your toast?" his eyes twinkled with laughter. "Your father is outside and your mother is at the church getting ready for the women's fellowship."

Serena instantly forgot the reason for her rush to exit the back door. She noticed the bouquet of fresh flowers, and a bowl of fresh sliced fruit on the breakfast table. Ike cut the omelet in half and placed two breakfast plates on the table.

"Coffee or juice?" he asked, feeling quite at home in Gladys' kitchen. "Girl, come on, sit down, and eat before my specialty omelet gets cold."

Serena could hear her stomach growling. She took the seat across from Ike. "I'll take juice," she replied awkwardly.

It was enough that she had discovered Edgar sitting out in front of her parent's house. Now, here was Ike, looking very much at home in their kitchen. She was the one feeling like a guest. This was too much for a Saturday morning.

"So how does it feel to return to the eagle's nest?" Ike asked, placing a glass of apple juice in front of Serena.

Ike found the setting quite comfortable and so far it was unfolding very well. He had hoped Serena would come out before he had finished and gone on about his day. Sam and Gladys had practically abandoned him to the house hoping that breakfast would get them together.

"It's interesting," Serena offered. "Will you say grace or shall I?" she asked.

"I'll be glad too," Ike responded easily. "This is something to be thankful for on this Saturday morning. Usually, on Saturday mornings about this time, I'm on the job filling up on a cup of coffee and donuts."

They both bowed their heads while Ike offered grace. Serena enjoyed his flow of words and the ease in which he spoke so freely to God. There was nothing false or pretentious about this man. He had a confidence in his newly found relationship with God that one would think he'd had for years.

"For a minute there, I thought you didn't take very kindly to seeing me in your parent's kitchen," Ike stated between eating cheese grits, and a couple slices of bacon he had placed on their plates. "You looked a little disturbed when you entered."

Serena had taken several bite size portions of her omelet and was thoroughly enjoying the taste. "Oh, not at all," she wiped the corners of her mouth. "I was a little preoccupied with all the activity going on outside my window. I'm not used to this much early morning activity."

"Well, we've been at it since six o'clock," Ike replied. "I helped your father replace some ceiling bulbs at the church. Then we put some new hinges on a few doors. I cut the church's lawn while he trimmed the shrubbery. About that time, the women began to set up for their meeting. I came over here and Mama Gladys put me to work wrapping muffins and brownies. She left and then Mr. Sam suggested that I conjure up some breakfast."

"Somebody should have wakened me," Serena fussed, finishing up the rest of her omelet. "I told Mother that I would take care of wrapping the baked goods."

"I think she wanted you to get your rest. She seems to think you're under a lot of stress right now."

Ike eyed her curiously wondering just what was going in this lady's life. She seemed to have everything working in her favor. What possibly could have made her come back home? How long would it take for her to get over the whatever? Or should he say whomever?

Serena sighed heavily hanging on to Ike's last statement. "I don't want to burden my parents with my troubles. They will just stress themselves unnecessarily. You know to the point of worry, and that's the last thing I want them doing, worrying about me. So I just tell them enough. You understand my position, don't you?"

"Of course," Ike replied, refreshing his cup of coffee and Serena's juice glass. "You guys have a pretty cool relationship. I don't think they're going to press you for details. I'm sure they're going to watch over you and read you like a book until you decide to leave the nest again."

Serena nodded her head in agreement. "Well, at the rate things are going now, I think I've become an open book to everyone who calls and dials this number. Why do people always think there has to be a crisis for someone to return home? Maybe, I just wanted to come home for the interest of my parent's welfare." Maybe, I see a need to be with my parents in their senior years."

"That's right and it sounds believable," Ike said, trying to be encouraging.

Serena got up to put her empty plate and glass in the sink. "Well, that's the reason I'm giving for inquiring minds that feel the need to be in other folk's business."

Ike gave out an amused laugh and finished off the last of the cheese grits. He had wanted to say that he was definitely one of the inquiring minds that wanted to know. He wanted to know the real reason for her retreat to the safety and security of her parent's watchful eye.

"Ike, thanks for breakfast and that was a very tasty omelet," she gave him a soft warm smile, collected his empty plate, and took it to the sink. "But, the next time I want the whole omelet," she laughed.

"Will there be a next time?" Ike asked from his seated position at the table. His tone was casual, but this was the most serious inquiry he had made all morning.

Serena felt his eyes searching her for a response that was deeper than the question he'd asked. Startled, she felt a heart-warming tremor going through her whole body. Her heart was pounding, and she sensed the feeling of something deep passing between them. She glanced away quickly.

"I'm sure it will. I know you can tell by now that you're the son my parents never had."

"That's a good thing," Ike stated, collecting the dirty cooking utensils scattered around the countertop and putting them in the sink. "Well, they're the parents I never had in a traditional two parent home such as this."

For a few minutes and in silence they both washed and dried the breakfast dishes. Sensing the warmth of each other's closeness, they were both thinking how this Saturday was really getting off to a great start.

"Well isn't this a cozy sight," Sam stated, entering from the back door. "I could spell that bacon clear across the street. I just knew it could wake up the living dead."

Serena welcomed her father's big wide grin knowing that whatever scheme he had setup had worked. She smiled and handed him her drying towel.

"I guess I'm the living dead that you're referring to?" she said humorously. "Gentlemen, I'm going over to the church to see how things are shaping up for the fellowship."

"Don't leave on my account," Sam stated. "I'm just passing through for a minute. Go on and finish up with what you were doing and talking about."

"And I'm sure you would just love to know what we were talking about," Serena laughed, kissing her father on the cheek and hurrying out the back door.

Ike and Sam talked for a few minutes longer. Ike walked across the street and got into his car. It was already after ten o'clock and the visiting women circles from other churches had start gathering for the fellowship event.

Ike watched Serena as she stood outside and talked with some of the ladies. "Oh God, what a lovely vision she is," he thought silently. He watched her for a minute and wondered what had just happened on this Saturday morning.

Would he ever have a chance to cook breakfast for her again? What was that intense feeling that passed between them? He was certain she felt it. It had been too intense for her not to have felt it. What was going on with Serena and why was she returning home after all these years? How long should he wait before trying to discover her level of interest in him? Could this just all be his imagination and internal desires of wanting something more in his life? Or was it just something to satisfy his sexual desires? To these questions he had no answers. But, he felt as though he had just experienced one of the most memorable days in his life.

"Come on Lord, send your blessing. I need a blessing. She needs a blessing. We all need a blessing."

"I would like to order a plant for the best manager in the world," Dimples spoke into the speakerphone. "A large peace lily sounds nice," she responded to the florist. "Just sign the card *Ike's Team* and invoice the corporate account. Delivery in an hour would be perfect."

Dimples twirled around in Ike's chair at his office desk. There were neat stacks of file folders labeled with sticky notes for reminder and action. She was amazed at how organized and efficient Ike had become. At first, he had required a lot of assistance with staying on top of deadlines, performance reviews, check rides, and other time sensitive reports. Now, he was organized and on top of things. Ike was definitely corporate management material and his future was destined for higher level positions.

Ordering the plant had been a suggestion from Ike's workgroup. She brought a card and everyone signed their appreciation to the best manager that they've had in a long time. She was proud that Ike was her friend and church member. She had been here for him since his first day at the station. And, if her prayers were answered, maybe she would be his woman of choice. But, that was something she would have to approach lightly.

Ike was like a nervous stallion just before a race at any mention of the word commitment and marriage. He would be ready to bulk and run if he even suspected that she was hoping that they would become a couple. She would just have to guide things along until he realized that she was the woman he needed.

"I've done my work here," Dimples smiled. "He'll know that I ordered it, and he'll be sure to come looking for me when it arrives."

Observing a picture of Ike with his mother and sister, on a bookshelf across from his desk, she gave it a quick glance. She made a mental note to place a picture of the two of them next to it. This would be the first official announcement that they had become a couple.

"I'm going to use every trick in the book, I'll try my best to get you hooked...oh baby, 'cuz every minute and hour, I'm going to shower you with love and affection....look out boy,....I'm coming in your direction...oh baby! I'm going to make you love me, ooooh baby...," she hummed happily, closing his office door behind her.

Clarice Webb had missed Ike more than she thought possible in the last few months. His weekly telephone call came every Sunday evening and his monthly envelope was like clockwork. She could count on him to send her a financial package.

"Ike, I ain't no charity case," she stated through teary eyes. "I'm making it and I always have and I always will."

"Mama, you are my charity case," Ike laughed. "Stop acting like you got a bank account. I know what you got coming in. Since your old man is on his last leg, you need all the help you can get. This is Foxy Fox's boy you're talking too, remember?"

Ike always made her laugh when he would call himself Foxy Fox's boy. "I'm by myself now. Didn't I tell you that I put his sorry butt out? I still don't believe that you done went and got yourself all saved, sanctified, and holy on me. I tell you, Marlene is driving me crazy with her prim and proper self. She ain't pushing the religion, but she sure is working my nerve with her uppity self."

"Okay, Mama, just cut back on the beer and cigarettes. That's all we're asking you to do. It's a health concern. In the meantime, me and Marlene are praying for things to come together for your good."

Clarice dried her teary face. "Mr. Big Time Manager, you take time out to come see us. We ain't seen you since you got baptized. How is everyone in Memphis? Are you dating anyone special yet?"

Her conversations with Ike would always end on that note and he would find her questions amusing. He never responded with a definite answer on his love interests. He always left her feeling hopeful that it would be soon and she would be the first to know.

Marlene called Clarice more than she visited. Clarice didn't spend much time with her grandchildren because

Marlene disapproved of the smoke and beer drinking at Clarice's home. Marlene would only let them visit if Clarice promised that she would keep her friends away while the children were visiting.

"You can't save them from the world," Clarice shouted at Marlene through the telephone. "I don't plan on changing any time soon. So you might as well let them see me and love me just the way I am."

"Mama, you don't even try to do better," Marlene screamed back. "And, when you get sick, I'm the one who has to see about you. Can't you just at least lay off the beer and cigarettes for your own good health?"

"Look girl, is you or ain't you bringing my grandchildren over here? Stop giving me all that yackety-yack. You know I'm here by myself, and you don't have to worry about my grandchildren seeing me with no man. I raised you and Ike, and y'all came out pretty decent. You're the one who's going to drive me crazy," Clarice fussed.

Marlene's heart would always soften and she would leave the kids overnight. Clarice would go the distance the entire visit by not smoking and drinking. She didn't want the little reporters going back home telling Marlene, and she never wanted to cut herself off from Marlene and the kids. She needed and wanted them in her life.

Ike was pleasantly surprised when he saw the plant and card in his office after a stressful staff meeting at corporate headquarters. The plant and card had Dimples' touch all over it. Dimples had gone by the time he got through checking in  the evening couriers. They were a good group to manage and he enjoyed providing the leadership for his workgroup.

Even though it meant he had to jump in a truck and deliver packages along with them. He attempted to call Dimples on her cell phone and at her home. He made a mental note to thank her at church later on that night.

The services had already started when Ike came in through the side door. When the ushers opened the door, he quickly found his way down front to where he knew Samuel Garrett would be sitting. Sam's face lit up when he saw him coming. The two embraced and Sam never missed a beat in shouting up praise.

Ike focused his attention towards the pulpit, but his glance went directly to the soprano section to catch a glimpse of Serena. Her head was down and Dimples caught his eye and gave him a smile. He smiled back warmly thinking of the beautiful plant.

Pastor Kenton delivered a powerful sermon. Just before Pastor Kenton gave the invitation to discipleship, Mack Earl found his way down front and indicated he was going to sit on the front bench. Pastor Kenton nodded in agreement. Ike moved aside to make room for Mack Earl and gave him a strong handshake. Everyone was surprised when Mack Earl stayed planted between Sam and Ike.

After the benediction, Ike took a few minutes to fellowship with Mack Earl. Exiting the building, shaking hands, and chatting with members took up quite a bit of his time. By the time he came out the front entrance, he could see Serena crossing the street with Sam and Gladys.

He spotted Dimples talking with another choir member. Ike made his way over to Dimples. "Nobody's gathering for a late snack tonight," he grinned. "I was hoping to join in for the fellowship."

"Not tonight," Dimples responded. "It's once a month now. I think we were beginning to put on some unnecessary pounds. It's the last Wednesday in the month."

The other choir member said goodnight and left Dimples and Ike standing on the sidewalk.

"Thank you for the plant," Ike grinned. "I know my group of package moving animals didn't think of it by themselves."

"You'll be surprised," Dimples laughed, touching him lightly on the shoulder. "It was one of them that suggested it. They just needed a little help in getting it ordered."

"Dimples, thank you for all that you've done to keep me organized. I couldn't have made it without your help."

"Well, you're so efficient now until you don't even ask me to help you anymore. What's up with that?"

"You're a good teacher," he laughed. "I can't stay dependent. You know that male power thang. Me man....me do it by myself."

They laughed and continued to talk for a few minutes longer. Sam was coming back from across the street ready to lock up the church.

"Y'all go on home now. Working folk need to be in bed this time of night," he shouted over to Ike and Dimples.

"Is Serena coming back out?" Dimples inquired. "She's the reason I'm standing out here."

"I don't think so. She's seeing after her mother. Gladys isn't feeling well," Sam voiced just before disappearing into the church.

Ike's heart dropped in disappointment when he heard Sam's response. He wouldn't get to see Serena. He didn't dare go over there and interrupt. He and Dimples headed towards the back of the church to their parked cars. They both were thinking to themselves that they would have to call and check on Gladys the next day.

Serena peeped through the window from her room with the light outs. She watched Ike and Dimples. They made a handsome couple. She knew Dimples was crazy about Ike, and it would break Dimples' heart if Ike didn't feel the same way.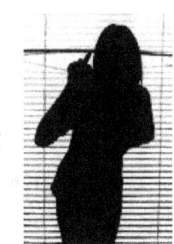

Surely, her emerging feelings for Ike were imaginary. Maybe, this was a form of transferring her feelings for Edgar over to the next available male who showed the slightest amount of attention or concern for her. Her heart was still in love with Edgar. Or was it?

Clarice's remarks were always in the back of her mind about how Ike didn't look at Dimples the way he looked at her. What did Ike's mother know anyway? Clarice should be the last opinion that anyone listened to when it came to a committed relationship. Or should Clarice's opinion be the first to be considered. She was extremely wise to the ways of the world and men.

"Oh well," Serena thought turning from the window. "I don't need to be talking about falling in love with nobody. I need my own personal psychiatrist right about now," she stated softly.

"Lord, you're my physician. Heal me. Send me what I need and send it with a quickness."

The insistent ringing of Ike's phone woke him from a very pleasant dream. He glanced over at the clock hoping it wasn't a third shift manager calling him to come in. The clock flashed *3:00*.

"Marlene, what's wrong? Is everything alright?" his sleepy voice came through the telephone.

Marlene's voice was all choked up and Ike could barely understand her words. "Ike, Mama's in the hospital. She called 911 and now they're talking about emergency surgery and she might not make it. Ike, I'm scared," she cried.

Ike jumped out of the bed. "What? How long has she been in the hospital?" he inquired, hitting the light switch.

"She just got here," Marlene sniffed. "She called me and said she was having chest pains and she was calling 911. When I got to the house they had put her in the ambulance. The doctor is saying she needs surgery...there may be blockage....I think Mama had a heart attack."

Ike's thoughts were racing. It would take him about three hours to drive to Birmingham. "Marlene, I'm heading out right now," he stated calmly. "I'll be there in a few hours. Call me on my cell phone. Just pray and keep yourself together. Mama's going to be all right. I just believe in my heart God ain't ready to take her yet."

Marlene felt calmer just hearing his voice and knowing that he was on the way to Birmingham. "Keep your cell phone on and be careful," she cried.

"I will and you be strong. Do what's needed on that end. I'll be there soon."

He pulled a duffle bag from the closet and packed a pair of slacks, casual shirts, and dress shoes. He grabbed his toiletries and threw them into the bag. It only took him a few minutes to put on a jogging suit and tennis shoes before he headed out the door. Without hesitation, he dialed Sam to let him know what was going on.

"Mr. Sam," Ike's voice sounded anxious. "I'm sorry to call you this early in the morning, but I've got an emergency. I'm leaving for Birmingham. My mother is in the hospital. She's had a heart attack and they're talking about doing heart surgery."

Sam responded the minute he heard Ike say his mother was in the hospital. "Look son, come by here and pick me up. I'll make that ride with you. No sense in you going by yourself this time of morning."

"I'll be fine," Ike said calmly. "I wanted you to know so that you can be praying. Also tell Pastor Kenton and the church family. I'll update you the minute I get there."

Serena had heard the phone ringing and picked up on the extension in her room. "Ike, I'm going with you," her voice came through loud and clear. "Daddy you stay here with Mother. She really needs to see the doctor herself on today. Ike, come and get me. It will take me just a few minutes to throw some things in a bag."

"Are you sure?" Ike asked. "I didn't call to interrupt y'all schedules. It's a kind gesture but I'll be fine."

Serena was already on her feet and pulling a small luggage bag out of the closet. "It will take you about fifteen minutes to get here and we can hit I-240 from this end. I'll be on the front porch waiting."

The phone went click on Serena's end while Sam and Ike were still connected. "I think you got a rider," Sam responded. "Son, you'll need her. It'll take her mind off her problems. Plus, she'll come anyway, with you or by herself."

"Yes sir," Ike sighed. "Mr. Sam, pray for my mother. About all I can say right now is Lord have mercy."

"That's a good prayer. You just keep saying Lord have mercy. He hears our every cry and call."

True to her word, Serena was standing on the front porch with her father at her side. Sam took her bag to the car and gave Ike a strong embrace.

"Be strong. Clarice is going to need you. I just got faith that everything is going to be all right."

"Thanks, Mr. Sam…..just pray for us."

Serena got in on the passenger side and fastened her seat belt. Ike pulled the car out of the drive and headed towards the highway. It felt right that she should be at his side. He gave her a warm smile.

"Thanks," he said warmly. "I'm good for the driving. You do the talking and we'll be there before we know it."

"I can handle that," she smiled back at him. "Ike, before we get on the highway, we need to say a prayer."

"Sure," Ike replied, pulling into a vacant lot. "Prayer is always in order and it's exactly what we need."

They held hands. Serena prayed for Clarice's healing and for Marlene and Ike's strength and courage to face whatever God had willed in this situation. She prayed for safe traveling and a peace of mind in all things.

"It is done," Ike whispered in confirmation.

"Yes, the Lord's will, will be done," she sighed. "Let's ride Mr. Package Express Man."

"Maybe you should give Dimples a call when we get to Birmingham. She can tell everyone at the office. There is no sense in waking her now. She'll worry and I'm sure she would appreciate the sleep," Serena added thoughtfully.

Ike glanced at his watch and agreed with her totally. "Yes, it's too early to wake Dimples, but not too early to give my Senior Manager a call," he responded, while hitting speed dial. He left an urgent message on his manager's machine stating he would be out for a few days due to his mother's condition. He would call back to give an update.

"I'll also give one of my couriers a heads up," he added. "They'll be arriving in a couple of hours."

Ike dialed another number and spoke with his employee. Serena focused her view on the horizon. It had been a long time since she had gotten up early to see the dawning of a new day.

"Earth to Serena....earth to Serena," Ike kept repeating. "Are you sleeping with your eyes wide open?"

"No, I'm awake," Serena stammered, coming out of a daze. "I guess I just got caught up in the beautiful horizon. It is so serene and peaceful this time of morning."

"We'll see the sunrise shortly," Ike stated softly. "That's my favorite time of the morning. Do you mind if I put on some music?"

"No, not at all. Do what makes you comfortable. You're the driver," she stated while adjusting her seat to a comfortable position.

Ike flipped open the music compartment and pulled out an instrumental contemporary Christian cd. Serena browsed his cd's and was quite impressed with the collection. Smooth jazz, classical, and gospel along with a few Natalie Cole and Will Downing disks.

"I like your music," she said holding up a Natalie Cole disk. "Have you read her autobiography *Angel on My Shoulder?*"

"I didn't do a lot of reading in my past lifestyle," Ike laughed. "Did you read it? I like that title."

"Twice and plus it's a movie," Serena laughed. "I'm one of her fans and a member of her online message board."

"So you're off into message boards and online stuff," Ike laughed. "You've got to educate me on that."

For the next hour they talked comfortably about music and their favorite celebrities. They both took in the beautiful sunrise. Ike was glad for the conversation. It kept his mind from thinking the worse about his mother's condition.

Marlene called to say that Clarice was in ICU and that the surgery was set for early afternoon.

"She's going to be alright," he glanced over at Serena with thanksgiving in his heart. "God is about to do a change within my mother. He ain't through with her yet. That was my grandmother's prayer. My grandmother told me before she died that God was going to pick her child up, turn her around, and place her feet on solid ground. She said she may not see it in her lifetime, but that me and Marlene would. I've been holding on to that prayer."

Serena was touched by Ike's sincere words. She had grown fond of Clarice in the short time that she was in her company. "Ike, I got a feeling that she's going to be alright too. Weeping may endure through the night but joy cometh in the morning."

"I like that," Ike smiled. "Plus, it's scriptural."

They resumed their conversation and the time seemed to fly by. The three hour drive was just about over when Ike pulled off the highway to refuel and check in with Marlene. A half hour later they were pulling into the St. Joseph's Hospital parking lot in Birmingham.

"I had a feeling he would bring you," Clarice stated, looking over at Serena. Her voice sounded weak and Serena could barely hear her. "You know it's true what 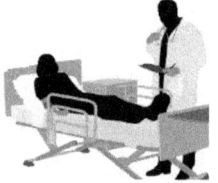 they say about seeing your life flash before your eyes. I just knew I was a goner. I saw just about everything in my life but a funeral."

"Miss Webb...I mean Clarice," Serena whispered while holding her hand. "Just rest. You don't have to keep talking to me."

"But I want to talk," Clarice stated. "I saw a wedding...it was all white and blurry. Couldn't see no faces but I knew it was a wedding. I was floating and feeling very happy."

"That was the anesthesia and meds," Serena laughed. "You've been waking up and drifting off to sleep since your surgery two days ago."

"Yeah, I know. I know Ike is gone to get some sleep at Marlene's house and they left you here with the patient."

"You gave us quite a scare," Serena stated.

"Raise my head up some," Clarice requested. "I'm ready to wake up and feel like myself again."

Serena handled Clarice with care and genuine concern until she was comfortable. Clarice was pleased with her assistance. She felt like talking more.

"I knew it was a heart attack...felt it coming," Clarice sighed. "Serena, before it hit, I called on God and my dead Mama to come and see about me. I think I repented, baptized myself, and joined somebody's church right there in my living room before I called 911. Hell, I wanted to live!"

"We want you to live too," Serena laughed.

"I heard y'all discussing my future. Seems like I'm going to Memphis to stay with Isaac for a while. But, I don't plan on being no burden to him. And, while I'm there I'm going to make sure you two get hitched up."

Serena was speechless. She had no response for that statement. "I'm calling the nurse to check your vitals," Serena replied. "You're feeling much better."

She called for the nurse and they spent the next hour getting Clarice's IV's unhooked and freshening her up. By the time Marlene and Ike arrived Clarice had eaten a light meal and had taken a nap. Serena reviewed the day's activities and reports from the doctors. Later that evening, Serena and Marlene left to get a full night's sleep. Ike was left with patient duty.

"Ike, I done seen the light," Clarice laughed. "Y'all don't have to worry about me smoking and drinking anymore. I want to live, and I know I got to make some serious changes in my lifestyle."

Ike was overjoyed. "Mama, that's good news. Plus, we've decided that you should stay with me for a while. It would make me real happy if you came peacefully. I sure don't want a knock down drag out fight about it."

"Boy, you ain't got no fight here. None of this is going to be a cake walk, but I'm ready to make a change. Maybe, the second half of my life will be my best years. I just heard somebody on the television say that their latter years will be their best years. It sounded good to me."

"Yes Mama," you know you are quoting scripture."

"The heck I am," she laughed. "I plan on quoting scripture, the pledge of allegiance, and anything else that will help me. One thing I plan on helping you quote, before God shut my lights out, will be some marriage vows."

Ike almost fell off the cot. He looked up to see if Clarice was hooked up to anything, but she wasn't. He was stunned. Clarice had a big smile on her face watching his reaction.

"You think I'm drugged up don't you?" she laughed. "Nope, I just know a man in love when I see it. You've had your eyes on Serena since I first seen you watching her. She punches all of your buttons. Maybe it took a heart attack to help me see life differently, but I know you're a changed man. Son, you need a wife."

Ike got out the chair and stood by her bed. He still didn't know what to say. He just knew that flesh and blood hadn't revealed that to his mother. It had to be spiritual.

"Say it ain't so," Clarice smiled. "And don't give me no double talk about it being that Dimples' girl. You're in love with Serena, and if you say it ain't so I'll put a defibrillator on both of y'all hearts. Tell me if I'm wrong, and if you do, you're just flat foot lying."

"Mama, I can't believe the words marriage and vows came out of your mouth. God must've given you a new heart, mind, and spirit when you were in surgery."

"You got that right," Clarice winked playfully. "Just don't tell anybody. Well, I guess you should tell Marlene.

She will probably pee in her pants. You know she loves me dearly, don't you?"

Ike kissed Clarice on the cheek and smiled. It was time to go home. His mother was going to be alright. He closed his eyes and thanked God.

"Surely God has smiled on us today. Thank you Lord!"

"Come on in Ike, the door isn't locked," Gladys responded. "How is Clarice doing?" she asked.

Ike entered the house and locked the door behind him. He was hoping to see Serena perched on her favorite chair. He suspected that she would be finalizing plans for the outreach meeting that was scheduled within the hour. But, Serena was nowhere in sight.

"Mama is fine and Marlene needs a break. She's counting the weeks for her to come to Memphis."

Gladys knew that Clarice was probably a handful, especially with her giving up cigarettes and beer. She and Sam called her weekly and she wouldn't let the call end until a prayer had been prayed on her behalf.

"I really admire her genuineness and honesty. There is nothing fake or phony about Clarice Webb," Gladys added thoughtfully.

Ike was anxious and excited. Serena was coordinating a project that would be helping to get men involved throughout the church and neighborhood. He was glad to participate. Plus, he had a strong desire to see Serena.

"Where is Serena? Has she already gone over to the church for the meeting?" he asked.

"No, that meeting was cancelled. Didn't you get a call from the committee's secretary?" Gladys asked.

Ike had five messages on his phone. "Well, I guess I should listen to them," he sighed. "Why was the meeting cancelled? Did Serena cancel it?"

"Yes she cancelled it and I don't know why. She left here like she was going to put out a fire or something. I thought she was headed over to the church until I saw her car pulling out the driveway. I was going to ask if you knew why?"

Ike took a seat and wondered if he should inquire about Serena's personal business. But, he knew whatever he wanted to know it should come from Serena.

"Well, here comes Sam." Gladys heard his truck coming into the driveway. "Maybe, he knows why she cancelled the meeting."

Gladys saw the disappointment on Ike's face when she stated Serena was not home. She was anxious to ask Ike a few questions, and hopeful that the past few weeks had produced two lovebirds. Sam was glad to see Ike's car in front of the house. He unloaded his shopping bags and came up front to the living room.

"Hey folks," he stated, giving Ike a handshake. "Serena's car is gone. Where is she? Don't I need to set up for that meeting tonight?"

"Serena cancelled the meeting and left out of here flying," Gladys responded. "She answered the phone and I thought she had won the lottery the way she lit up."

"She didn't say where she was going?" Sam inquired curiously. "Or why she cancelled the meeting? That's mighty strange."

"I think she was going to the university. She did say she wouldn't be too late returning and not to wait up for her," Gladys replied.

Gladys was watching Ike's expression. Suddenly, his beeping cell phone diverted his attention. It couldn't have come at a better time. The text message indicated that his 9:00 appointment was still on. He had purposely made it that late so that he could be in Serena's meeting.

"It looks like I can change the time of a prior commitment with one of my couriers," he stated. "He's got an interview and I'm giving him some coaching advice."

"That's right, help another brother up," Sam responded.

Ike walked toward the door with a disappointed look on his face. "When Serena gets back tell her to give me a call. I'll be just as curious and worried as y'all until she gets home."

"I'll write her a note to call you just in case I doze off," Gladys replied.

Gladys read him like a book. He seemed perplexed about Serena's actions. Why would she cancel a planned meeting at the last minute? Where could she have rushed off to after receiving a phone call? Who was on the other end?

"Good night Ike," Gladys and Sam both echoed each other while noticing his somber mood. "Come by tomorrow and get you some fresh cooked garden vegetables. We'll be waiting for you," Gladys added, hoping that tomorrow will give them some much needed answers.

Serena was quite perplexed. Edgar had called and insisted on them meeting. He said that he had good news and he needed to see her immediately. She asked to meet the next day, but he kept insisting. Then he threatened to come to her parent's home if  she didn't come. She hated calling off the outreach meeting but it seemed necessary to face Edgar tonight.

They were meeting at 7:30 at the Olive Garden on the other side of town. She wasn't hungry, but as usual, it had to be his way or no way. She had hurriedly changed into a fashionable sundress, matching accessories, and sling strap pumps. Edgar was always particular about what she wore. She questioned why she should bother but that much was still intact. She wanted to look her best so he could have a visual of what he didn't have anymore.

After pulling up on the parking lot and finding a parking space, she had another fifteen minutes to get herself together. Taking a quick glance in the mirror, she checked her lipstick and hair. Everything was in place and the reflection staring back at her was very striking.

"How can he still excite me? I shouldn't have come. I should have screamed get away from me Satan," she thought silently. "Come on and face your demon. You've come too far to turn back now."

Entering the restaurant she felt stronger about meeting him. Edgar Dupree was no longer her weakness. She knew with certainty that the life he offered was not her destiny. God had much more in store for her. Within seconds, she spotted Edgar as the waiter escorted her to a booth in the back.

"Ooh wee baby cakes, I want to squeeze you tight. You are glowing like a sweet beautiful peach," he whispered, giving her a warm hug.

Her heart was doing leap frogs. She wasn't as sure of herself seeing him face to face. He was looking handsome and wearing that cologne that made her melt in his arms.

"Edgar, what is this news that just couldn't wait?" she inquired hurriedly and sounding a little nervous. "I had to cancel something important."

"Can't we eat our salads first? You know how I love a good salad," he grinned. "I've ordered wine because we have something worth celebrating."

He was too confident. Whatever news he had she knew that he felt it was going to get them back together.

"I think I should decide if it's newsworthy enough for celebration. So tell me now."

"Okay, since we've had our little separation time, and I see you're determined to be all grown up about it, we'll do it your way."

He pulled from his pocket two envelopes and handed them to her. She could tell that one had the return address of a lawyer's office and the other was a travel agency's envelope. For a brief moment, she stared at the two envelopes. Just a few months ago she would have been the happiest woman on earth to see legal documentation of any kind from Edgar.

"Open them," he grinned. "It's what you've wanted all these years. I did it for you. I did it for us. We can be together now. Babycakes, I'm a free man."

Speechless, she continued to stare at the two envelopes. Her head was spinning. She felt confused. She didn't know what she wanted now.

"I'm sorry Edgar. This is too much, I've got to....." she stammered. "Excuse me.....I have to find the lady's room....this is just too much."

Hurriedly, she went to the lady's room.

Ike changed the meeting time with his employee to *8:00*. They both agreed to meet at the Olive Garden, which was on the same side of town that he lived. A salad and a glass of wine was just what he needed to take  the edge off his hunger and mood. He arrived on time and his employee was already seated and waiting.

"Brandon, since the church meeting got cancelled, I can really critique you now," Ike stated, giving him a firm handshake. "Let's eat first. I'm starving."

"I hear you, boss man," Brandon stated. He pulled out an impressive looking portfolio. "This is the one that I will leave with them after the interview."

"Quite impressive," Ike stated, reviewing the packet. "Look man, I know you got the jitters, but you've got to tighten up on a few of your responses."

The waiter placed breadsticks, salad, and water glasses on the table. Ike looked up and suddenly caught a glimpse of Serena walking towards a table. He was surprised to see her. A man immediately stood up as she approached him, and put his arms around her shoulders. He appeared to be comforting her. From a distance, she seemed to accept his embrace and sat snugly in his arms. Ike felt as if his heart had stopped beating. For a few minutes, he thought he had stopped breathing.

"Boss, are you alright?" Brandon asked. "You look like you just seen a ghost or something."

Brandon followed Ike's line of vision. "Do you know that couple? Is she somebody to you? I know that man. Boss, are you okay?"

Ike took a sip of water and kept his attention on the couple in the booth. He could hear Brandon's inquiries but he couldn't respond.

"You know that man?" Ike asked, finding his voice.

"Yep, he's some type of policeman or detective or something. His wife owns that pricey boutique downtown. The girl looks familiar to me also, but I can't place her right now. She better run because he's bad news."

Brandon had Ike's full attention. "Other than being married, why do you say that he's bad news?" Ike asked.

"From what I've heard he has a trail of broken hearts. His wife ain't nothing nice to tangle with either. You know that desperate housewife drama," Brandon laughed. "Come on boss man, talk to me, what's up? Who is the chick and what is she to you?"

Ike's heart was still on the floor. He was finally getting some information that he needed to know.

"She's just my church member," Ike responded. He noticed that Serena had pulled away from the man's embrace. They appeared to be having a heated conversation.

"Yeah, I know her," Brandon stated with excitement. "She's Dimples' girlfriend....Serena. I thought I knew her. What the heck is she doing with that buzzard? She must go for the older married type because she ain't gave none of us the time of the day."

"What do you mean by that?" Ike shifted his gaze to Brandon, staring him directly in the eye.

"Well, let me rephrase that," Brandon stammered. "First of all, I'm a happily married man. So it ain't my knowledge first hand. Dimples tried to hook her up with a couple of the guys at the station, but she wasn't interested. She didn't give them the time of the day. "

Ike anxiously rubbed his hand across his forehead. He didn't have any claim on Serena. She wasn't his girl. She was just his church member and a friend. True, he wanted a relationship, but he hadn't made that move yet. They were still at first base and just getting to know each other. It was very apparent that she wasn't completely over the who and what that forced her to move back home.

Suddenly, the thought of Dimples anticipating them becoming a couple ran across his mind. She hadn't come right out with it but he knew her game. Before he could move on with Serena, he needed to clear the air with Dimples. Serena probably didn't want her friendship with Dimples compromised as well. There were just too many twist and turns to be worked out before pursuing an exclusive dating relationship with Serena Garrett.

Ike felt agitated. "Come on Brandon, let's take this meeting to my house."

"I thought you were starving," Brandon frowned, feeling confused.

"I'll be more attentive at my place and I can really critique you then," Ike grinned, while placing a tip on the table. "That is the purpose of our meeting, right?"

"Yeah right," Brandon stood, placing his materials back into his briefcase. "I'm going to get the bad end of whatever is frustrating you. I see it coming."

"Exactly!" Ike grinned. "If you want to run with the big dogs, you got to learn how to bark. You best recognize and try to keep up."

Ike took one last glance at the couple. Serena seemed to be totally engrossed and unaware of anything else. Ike was certain that he wouldn't be a distraction to the couple in the booth in the back of the restaurant.

Serena's teary eyes staring back at Edgar revealed her deep emotions concerning the envelopes that he had presented her.

"Edgar, this is not what I want anymore. There was a time I would have sold my soul to the devil to see this happen. I don't want to be the reason you leave your wife and family. I don't want that travesty hanging over my head."

Edgar was shocked. He took several swallows of wine before he could respond.

"Woman, you've lost your mind! You put me through hell, and now you say this isn't what you want. You don't know what you're saying. Do you know how much I'm giving up for you? Baby, it ain't no turning back now. Your name is all over these divorce papers."

Serena looked extremely fragile. The more she looked at Edgar the more she realized that he represented a part of her life that she wanted to cast into the pit of hell. Struggling for composure and self-control, she searched for the words to articulate her feelings.

Through teary eyes she spoke. "Edgar, how dare you lay the total blame on me for our affair. I'm just one of the many links in your chain of fools. You're not giving up nothing for me. It's all about you and what you want for yourself. So don't give me this line of bull that it's all my fault. If my name is anywhere on those papers, I suggest you include all the other fools who fell in your trap. If you don't, I can, and I will. You will be exposed for the womanizer and adulterer that you truly are."

Edgar ignored Serena's accusations and focused more on her vulnerability. It wasn't in his best interest to challenge her statements because she was right. He hadn't given her name, but his wife had somehow found her name. She had put Serena's name in the divorce petition.

"Look Serena," he smiled nervously. "You're upset and obviously my news is just too overwhelming. Baby, I know this is a surprise, but you've got to get beyond your guilt and emotions. You didn't think this was going to be pretty with a fairy tale ending, did you? This is the reality of what we've been doing for the past four years. That's the reason for the second envelope. We can get away and enjoy ourselves on a Caribbean island before dealing with this mess. Baby cakes, I am doing this for you."

Serena closed her ears and heart to Edgar's words. She silently prayed that God would forgive her and provide a way out from this evidence of her sinful life. When she spoke again, she was surprised at her composure.

"Edgar, we've both sinned. Now our sins have come to the light. I'll answer to my part, but I will not continue in this adulterous affair with you. I ended it and I didn't give you any hope of us getting back together. I didn't ask you to do this. Maybe, in past years I begged for it, hoped, wished and even prayed that you would leave your wife for me. Yes, I feel guilty, ashamed, and sorrowful. I suggest you go back home and try to save your marriage. You see, I have a different prayer now. I pray that God will send me a husband that I can call my own."

Consumed with his unchecked emotions, Edgar snatched up the two envelopes and placed them back into his pocket. Seething with anger, he wanted to lash out and hurt her with more than just his words.

"Look Serena, I'm going to leave before I do something that will land me in jail. I thought you wanted this divorce. I'm giving you a new life on a silver platter and you're too sanctimonious to see what you're turning down. Baby, where was all this religion when you were playing house with me for four years? But don't worry, there are plenty more women out there just waiting for what you're turning down. Don't come back crying and begging for me to come back to you. Hear me loud and clear, and let there be no misunderstanding, this time it's really over. I'm ending it this time. Go on and find that husband to call your own. But, baby girl, you'll never find another like me. Try to have a good life, if you can."

Edgar stood up and tossed a hundred dollar bill on the table. He walked off and never looked back. Tears streamed down her face. She felt sad for his wife and children. She felt sad for the life of secrecy and sin she'd lived for four years. But, now she rejoiced, and her tears were joyful. She was thankful that it had truly ended. She was thankful that she had had enough strength to walk away completely. She was thankful that God had given her a way of escape.

She knew Edgar well enough to know that he had been pissed off from her rejection. His pride would never let him approach her again. She beckoned for the waiter and requested that he prepare the two untouched dinner entrees, salads, and breadsticks for carry out.

"Do you care for an unopened bottle of wine?" the waiter asked. "Compliments from us to you."

"That will be wonderful," she smiled at the Italian waiter. She knew others had witnessed her and Edgar's raw emotions and verbal exchange.

Serena walked to her car in the pleasant night air with a peaceful spirit. She had two full carryout bags, a bottle of wine, and an envelope for two future complimentary dinners.

"Indeed this has been a celebration," she sighed. "My life is changing for the better."

Ike's clock was flashing *8:55*. He was feeling very moody and irritable. The coaching session with Brandon had been brief and effective. His thoughts were consumed with Serena and her date at the restaurant. The ringing of his cell phone snapped him back. He answered on the first ring.

"Hey Ike, can you talk?" Serena inquired.

"Yes," he sighed, feeling relieved to hear her voice. "What's going on? Are you okay?"

"No," she replied softly. "I'm outside in your parking lot. I've got dinner for two if you're hungry. I sure could use a listening ear."

Ike was surprised and could hardly contain his excitement. "Sure, I'll come down and get you."

He hung up before she could respond. She had only been to his place once. It was for a fellowship that Dimples had hosted when he first moved into his condominium.

Ike sprinted around in his living room gathering up work manuals and newspapers. He was feeling very thankful because things seemed to be working out for the good. He was anxious to learn more about Serena's truths and the matters of her heart.

By *10:00* they had finished the carry-outs and casual conversation about his job and living in Memphis. She admired the design and décor of his condo. Ike noted that she appeared relaxed and not in any hurry to disclose anything about her evening at the restaurant.

"I'm going to leave this wine with you," Serena smiled. "I had a glass earlier and one glass is enough for me."

"I'll save it for another special occasion," Ike laughed.

"Well, aren't you going to inquire why I'm here with dinner and wine?" she asked.

"The ball is in your court. When you're ready to tell, I'm ready to listen."

Serena took in a deep breath and exhaled. She started with the telephone call that caused her to cancel the outreach meeting. She told how she had spent the last four years living a life of secrecy and adultery.

Ike listened with his ears and his heart. In return, he told her all about his former lifestyle. Neither judged the other as they talked about repentance and desiring new lifestyles. They were both praying for new beginnings.

Ike didn't mention that he'd seen her at the restaurant. She deserved her privacy. She had proved to be honest and full of integrity. Close to midnight, he walked her to the car. It felt natural and very good when he embraced her in a warm and heartfelt hug. He could feel the rhythm of her heartbeat and it seemed to be beating as fast as his. He wanted more. He wanted to kiss her and hold her longer. But, it wasn't time. He released her and watched her drive away.

"Lord, this is definitely a job for you," he thought silently. "Both of us need grace and mercy in a special way."

Serena promised to call him the minute she pulled into her driveway. She could still feel his arms around her and the beat of his heart in rhythm with hers. There was no denying that something was developing between them. She wanted more and desired more with Cecil Isaac Webb.

"Oh Lord, why is this feeling like another tangled web that is being weaved?" she sighed.

The smell of fresh brewed coffee lured Serena out of a pleasant sleep and into the kitchen with her parents. Despite her late night, she felt renewed and energized.

"Where did you go last night rushing from here like a bat out of hell?" Gladys asked anxiously over morning coffee.

"I had a little business I had to handle," Serena winked playfully at her mother. "I see y'all didn't burn the midnight oil waiting up for me, which is a major improvement."

"Don't be sassing me. I wasn't sitting up waiting but I was waiting. Did you see my note to call Ike?"

Serena's smile was as bright as the sun coming through the window. Just the mention of Ike's name made her feel cheerful. She wanted to tell her Mother about her evening but that would mean revealing too much information. She wasn't ready to divulge everything, at least not just yet. For right now, it was best to keep her developing feelings about Ike to herself.

"Yes Mother, I'll talk with him later today."

"It would be nice if you would pursue a long term relationship with someone rather than another degree," Sam spoke over the newspaper that he was reading.

"Daddy, why that conversation at the mention of Ike's name?" she grinned. "You think that Ike and I could be more than just good friends? Anyway, Dimples has her eye on him. What kind of friend would I be?"

Gladys could have danced a jig for this opportunity to voice her opinion. "Serena, you would have to be a blind person to not see how he acts when you're around him. He lights up like a Christmas tree. And, since I know you so well, I know you try your best not to show any emotions. As a matter of fact, you try so hard until it's obvious."

"Oh Mother," Serena laughed. "You need to pursue writing romance novels. You're bubbling over with stuff."

"As a matter of fact, I may just write one. You two go ahead and work out the ending because that's all we need is the perfect ending."

"Daddy, when you see Mom's doctor today, be sure to get her some medicine for being an old romantic. And, get an extra prescription for yourself."

Sam folded the paper and cleared the breakfast table. "You're feeling very happy this morning," he said kissing Serena on her cheek. "I like it when my baby girl is happy."

She wanted to share just how happy she was feeling, but that would mean telling them the whole sordid mess. And, to mention Ike in the testimony would be premature. Her feelings for him were becoming very real, but she didn't know how he felt about her. From all indications, she was just a good friend on the list with his other good friends.

Plus, it was obvious to everyone that Dimples wanted him. And frankly, she was just too unsure of being in love anymore. She thought she had loved Edgar but look how that played out. Maybe, her feelings for Ike were just a rebound interest. Or was it love? Or was it just pure lust?

Ike also seemed happier than usual. Later that day, while toweling dry from a late morning shower, he couldn't stop smiling. His thoughts drifted back to last night with Serena. There were a couple of times that he just wanted to stop talking, take her in his arms, and kiss her long and hard. Lately, he had gotten his share of hugs and kisses on the cheeks, but he hadn't seriously kissed a woman or been sexually active since moving to Memphis.

Serena was stirring up desires that he hadn't let surface in nine months. Cold showers, a busy work schedule, and the challenging demands of being a manager had kept his mind focused and off of sex. Now, he was totally depending on being a new creation through his faith and belief in the word of God.

It was the insistent ringing of his house phone that changed his mood. Anybody who called him regularly knew to call him on his cell phone.

"Not interested," he answered thinking it was the telemarketers on their daily prowl.

"Hey Ike, where are you? I've been calling your cell phone and getting voicemail. You okay?" Dimples asked.

"Hey Dimples, I thought you were telemarketers calling. Yeah everything is just fine. Remember, I'm on second shift for the next few days. Didn't you read the memo?"

"Ike, that starts next week," she laughed. "See you still need me. It's a good thing I called you."

"No, I'm certain it's starts today. A revised schedule came out on yesterday. Look on my desk. Its right there on top, but thanks for looking out for me."

"My mistake," she apologized. "Why aren't you answering your cell phone? I've left two messages. One last night and one early this morning."

Ike went to the bedroom to get his cell phone. "Really, two messages, huh? I didn't hear it beeping. I hope Marlene hasn't tried to call. Hold on Dimples," he stated on the cordless phone.

He had two messages. He had put it on silent during last night's dinner and conversation with Serena. "Yeah....it is on silent. I see two messages," he confirmed.

"Again that just goes to prove that it's a good thing I am looking out for you," she laughed. "I've been trying to catch up with Serena since last night and she seems to be missing in action. I can't get an answer on their house phone or her cell phone. You know Mama Gladys wasn't feeling well. I wonder what's really going on?"

Ike listened and cleared his throat before speaking. He knew it would have to be sooner rather than later that he and Dimples had a heart to heart talk about their friendship. Now, with his feelings for Serena becoming more certain, he definitely needed to talk things out with Dimples.

"Dimples, put me down in your appointment book for lunch on tomorrow. I need your advice on a few things."

"Sure Ike," she responded. "I've already been thinking of ways to help when your mother gets here. You don't have to worry because you've got more support than you need."

"Thanks Dimples. That's very kind of you."

"Anything for you. You know I got your back," she whispered. "I've got calls holding. I'll call you back."

Ike listened to the hum of the dead line and held the phone. He noticed how the tone of her last comment had changed from casual to seductive. He suddenly felt compelled to tell Dimples that he was in love with Serena. But, he hadn't even told Serena that he was in love with her.

Why had this happened to him? There was a time he would have played them both and never given it a second thought. Now he was more concerned about Dimples' friendship with Serena than his desired relationship with

Serena. Had he suddenly developed a conscious? Was he on his way to being healed from his womanizing ways?

"Please, please, please Lord," he moaned out loud. "Help a brother out. All I know is that I want Serena Garrett to be my woman. I'm talking serious commitment with Serena. Lord, you're really going to have to work a miracle in this situation."

Serena stood in the long line wrapped around the building for early registration. Her thoughts were consumed with last night's dinner with Ike. The ringing of her cell phone brought her back into the present moment. Retrieving the phone from her bag, she saw that the call coming in was from Ike.

"Hello Isaac," she smiled.

"I'm just checking to see if you got up on time."

"What happened to my wake-up call, Mr. Early Morning Riser, huh?"

"See, that's why I'm calling," he grinned. "Remember, I set your cell alarm last night. I did my part."

Suddenly the line started to move and Serena found it difficult to talk. "Ike, I'm going to have to get back with you."

"Okay, remember I'm on second shift. So I'll give you a call later tonight if I'm not too busy. Is that okay?"

"Great...I'll be up late...," she hesitated. "I hope you aren't too busy with it being a new shift."

Ike didn't want to hang up the phone. He was tempted to come stand in line with her just to keep her company.

"Oh, I'm going to take time to call you," he responded. "Good luck on your class schedule."

Serena placed the cell phone back into her pocketbook. She let her thoughts drift back to their evening. She had felt very comfortable with him and found herself wanting to be more than just good friends. Several times she had to glance away for fear that he would see the desire in her eyes. The familiar feelings of being held, kissed, and making love filled her thoughts.

She enjoyed sex. She enjoyed being pleased and pleasing her man. Being with Edgar, and now being without him, was like dropping an addiction and going cold turkey. For four long years, she had believed that she couldn't live without the sex life that she had with him. But, the devil was a lie, and she wanted to be a living testimony of how God can bring you out of any situation.

At that moment and somewhere deep within her spirit, she truly desired to practice abstinence. "Oh Lord, give me strength. I'm not sure if I can do it. But, it is my heart's desire. So I pray this prayer, as I wait on you, please send me a husband that I can call my own."

The registration line had started to move again. "Hey lady, you're next," a young man from behind her shouted out. She moved quickly and found her assigned counselor. For the first time in a long time, she was feeling very much alive and like her old self again.

Dimples came over early to see Serena before Wednesday's night service. She wanted to find out why the outreach meeting had been canceled at the last minute.

"Girl, where were you last night?" Dimples asked anxiously, while Serena typed her fall schedule on her laptop. "We were ready to hear Ike's plans on canvassing the neighborhood. You know he just brings such a raw and exotic essence to everything."

"What do you mean by raw and exotic?" Serena looked up from her typing. "You make it sound like we're hosting a massage parlor or something. True, we need more men but those qualities are not needed in outreach and evangelism."

Dimples crossed her legs and admired her new candy apple red open toe pumps. "Honey baby child, those are two main ingredients in my areas of outreach. He needs to come on and reach out to me. If he don't hurry up, and make a move, I'm going to have to look at him in a different light."

Serena couldn't help but laugh at Dimples. Dimples had a hoochie side and no matter how she tried not to let it surface it always did.

"So, let me get this right. Your different light is that he may be gay?" Serena asked.

Dimples humorously clutched her chest and laid out on the couch. "Lawdy, lawdy, lawdy, if he is then just take me on the church grounds and shoot me. I'll be sick to my death. Girl, that man is just too fine not to be up in my bed."

Serena put away her laptop and joined her on the living room sofa. "Okay, Dimples, let's believe that he is one hundred percent heterosexual. Now, why does he have to be up in your bed?"

Dimples sensed a tone in Serena's voice that was unexpected. But, she felt gamed to play along. "Well, let's just state the facts. Since I ain't got no man, and you don't seem to be looking for one. I'm certainly not campaigning to get him up in some other woman's bed. I would think that I'm the best candidate. Wouldn't you agree, Miss Ma'am?"

Serena pondered her response for a minute. "Well, let's say I'm without a man and my name is in the pot also. I say he's fair game and may the best woman win."

"Good answer!" Dimples flashed a wide smirky grin. "Sounds like you want to be in the game."

Serena shifted her gaze away from Dimples. That was a statement she wasn't quite ready to answer. Dimples knew she had struck a nerve.

"Look Serena, it's been a while since we've had a heart to heart about your love life. My love life has always been an open book. I've respected your privacy, and I think I've been here for you whenever you reached out. So, tell me what gives with you and the mystery man, Edgar Dupree? Have you had your fill of him? Did he dump you? Did you dump him? Just give me the facts. Is it really over this time?"

Dimples had always gotten straight to the point. She had known about Serena's involvement with Edgar when it first started. She hated that Serena had let herself get caught up with a married man. She had gotten caught up with one too, but she hurried up and kicked him to the curb. She had begged Serena to do the same. Several times she had tried to hook her up with single guys from her job. But, Serena wouldn't love anybody but Edgar. She had hoped that Serena would come to her senses and walk away from her addiction to a man who she could never call her own.

Serena hugged a pillow close to her chest and curled up on the couch. "Yes Dimples, Edgar Dupree and I are done. We came to the end of the road for real on last night."

"Girl, why you didn't call me? I would've celebrated with you!" Dimples exclaimed moving closer to Serena on the couch. "Okay spill it. I know it's going to be good."

Serena cleared her throat and proceeded to tell Dimples about her evening with Edgar. "I really couldn't believe how good I felt when he walked out. I was so elated and thankful until I just had to tell somebody right then and there. So I called Ike because I knew he lived close by."

Dimples was surprised to hear Ike's name. "Ike.....Isaac Webb? You called him?" she asked in amazement. "Okay, okay, he lives around the corner from The Olive Garden. He could get to you sooner. I see the logic. But, why would you share something so personal with him. You don't know him well enough to share your darkest secrets."

Serena was slow to respond. "I called him because he lived around the corner. I was devastated and confused. I needed someone right then. And, Ike is my friend, and a Christian friend at that. It felt natural to call him."

Dimples sensed a slight headache coming on as she continued. "Yeah, you're right. Ike is a good listener and he certainly ain't no boy scout. I probably would've called him too. Girl, were you a basket case?"

Serena sighed with relief remembering how good it felt to share her liberation with Ike. "Oh no, I was alright when I called him. I felt like I had been set free. I hadn't felt like that in such a long time. That's why I'm certain, and I know, that I know, that Edgar Dupree is history in my life."

"So, did you tell Ike everything about you and Edgar?" Dimples asked cautiously.

"Not everything. He got the fact that I was with a married man. Do you think I should've not told him?"

"Ike is an open minded guy. I don't think he was playing checkers and holding his hands out there in the world," Dimples responded. "Well, he's finally gotten answers directly from you rather than asking around about your dating life."

Serena's eyes widened. "Ike's been asking around about me and whom I'm dating?"

"Yes," Dimples shrugged. "Girl, we might as well talk and open up before things get all crossed up."

"Before what get crossed up?" Serena sat up straight, feeling a little apprehensive about where the conversation was heading. "Seriously, do we need to talk about Ike?"

Dimple's tongue felt thick and heavy as she saw the need to explain her attraction to Ike. "Yeah, I should at least be honest with you about my feelings for Ike. Then, it'll be out in the open, and we'll both be on fair playing grounds."

"Fair playing ground! Wait just a minute," Serena scowled, sensing that this conversation was about to take a turn. "How is this turning into fair playing grounds for me and you over Ike? We're not competing for him."

Dimples paused and took a deep breath before speaking. "Serena, have you looked at Ike? I mean really looked at him. Ike is somebody that any woman would snatch up, take home, and put under lock and key. He's single, saved, career minded, making big dollars, and the door is wide open. I'm going to do my best to put my bid in and see who wins the prize. Wake up and get real, girlfriend."

Serena knew she had been out of the dating game for a while. And, she had no right questioning someone else's standards on getting a man. But surely, she wasn't out to outbid or win a man like he was a piece of meat on the auction block.

"Dimples, what happened to the man approaching you and finding you? The Bible says a man who findeth a wife finds a good thing. Not a woman who findeth a man finds a good thing."

"Now, I know you ain't quoting scriptures to me," Dimples laughed out loud. "I know you don't want me to go there with your hypocritical, in love with a married man, Mrs. Jones self. What kind of standard is that?"

It had been a long time since she and Dimples had had the kind of falling out that kept them from speaking to one another. The last time it happened, it had lasted for about four months, but they made up and became friends again.

Dimples' words cut deep. Serena knew she had made a valid point with the truth. She had no come back. Serena got up from the couch and checked the time. It was almost six o'clock and church started at seven. She  didn't feel like having a conversation that would end up with them hurting each other with harsh words. Somebody had to have some sense and put this conversation to rest.

"I need to get some food ready for Mom and Dad. They'll be home in a few minutes. Come on and help me get something warmed up and on the table."

Dimples gave Serena an apologetic look and followed her into the kitchen. "I'm sorry...," she said softly. "I didn't mean to go there and call you hypocritical. Serena, you know I'm passed that judgmental crap. Really, I'm sorry."

Serena sighed. "It ain't like you weren't telling the truth," she mumbled. "You know sometimes the truth hurts and it cuts deep. You just told the truth. I'm in no position to say nothing about nobody's lifestyle."

"Serena, since we're spilling the truth, I do need to tell you how I really truly feel about Ike. It needs to be said and out in the open. It's real talk about him being fair game for either one of us."

"Dimples, please," Serena turned to face her. "Let's not talk about Ike or any man. I don't know up from down. The last thing I need in my life is another love relationship."

"I hear you talking but I ain't buying it," Dimples retorted. "Look Serena, Ike has had his eyes on you since he first met you. I've been trying to get my hooks in him and the boy just ain't biting. Now, let me say this, so at least I can admit it, and move on with my life, okay?"

Serena took a seat at the kitchen table. Dimples stood by the refrigerator and stared out the kitchen window. Finally, she could tell the truth about her feelings for Ike.

"When he first joined the church, and we would talk at work, your name always popped up. He felt that you wasn't looking for a man. I told him you were already kind of involved. After a while he just stopped asking. When he stopped asking, I figured I might as well attach myself to him as a dear friend and coworker that he depended on for everything. Serena, you know that I come from a line of women who will use any crook or hook to get a man any way that we can. It didn't take me long to discover that Ike had been a womanizer in Birmingham and that he'd left a string of broken hearts behind him. When I found out the man didn't have any babies and baby mama drama going on, I knew he was somebody worth snatching up. So I figured, if I hung around long enough he would finally wear down, and come to me at least for his sexual needs. And, with his newfound spirituality, he'd see that I was enough woman for him. Eventually, we would hook up, marry, and live happily ever after. But so far, it ain't happened. What I do know is that the more he's around you, the more he is determined to wait you out. And now, that you've ended this thing with Edgar Dupree, and he knows it, you're fair game for him. If you don't want him then just be truthful and say so. I want him. And, if I can get him, I'm going to be with him. I don't need your approval to go after him either."

Dimples last statements took her by surprise. A brief and uncomfortable silence passed between them before Serena made direct eye contact with her. She could feel the corners of her mouth quivering.

"Dimples, I've never had any plans of being Ike's lady. All of this is happening too soon. I'm not fair game for anybody. I'm just a confused bundle of emotions right now. If I can make it through first semester of grad school, it'll be a miracle. I'm not going to lie and say that I don't have any interest in Ike. I do feel myself wanting to get to know him better. I am beginning to look at him differently. But, I can't allow myself to get involved with him or anyone. I need to be absolutely certain that I'm not on the rebound from Edgar. My heart can't take another relationship right now. Does that make sense?"

Dimples felt as though she had laid down a heavy load. Serena truly wasn't ready for a committed relationship with anyone. Dimples was certain that timing was everything in her interest to win Ike over. Ike was fair game. And, may the best woman win.

"Girl, believe it or not, I really understand," Dimples exhaled slowly. "Considering that you gave that man four years of unconditional love. It must've been some kind of crazy love. Just make sure Edgar Dupree is out of your system and pray it be quick. You're going to pass up one hell of a man if you walk away from Isaac Webb."

"So you think I should just hook up with Ike even though I'm still messed up about Edgar?"

"Girl, I'm just telling you the way it is," Dimples replied. "I do know this much for sure. I'm going to leave him alone for the time being for both of our sakes. But believe me, he is prime meat, and somebody is waiting in the cut for him, and they will snatch him up. He's being good but he ain't that good. Sooner or later, his sexual desires are going to get the best of him. And, the woman who gets him in her bed this time, will be the woman he will marry. Girl, you can take that to the bank."

Serena listened intently to Dimples advice. And, as usual, Dimples was on point. She also felt that Ike's sexual appetite was being constrained. She wanted to admit that he was fair game to any woman that desired him. She wanted to admit that she was relieved that Dimples would stop pursuing him. Because if any woman could wear him down, Dimples could do it. But, those were thoughts she would just keep to herself. If Ike was meant to be with her, fate would fix it, and it would work out for everybody's good.

Serena heard her father's truck in the driveway. She wasn't quite ready to end the conversation, but in a few minutes her parents would be inside. Any conversation about Ike was something that they enjoyed and welcomed.

She got up from the table and quickly embraced Dimples with an understanding hug. "Dimples, I'm really glad we talked. Let's just let it do what it's gonna do, and see how it all rolls out. I just pray that our friendship can stand up to any matters of the heart, and that Ike, or no man, will destroy it. I don't know what else to say or do. "

Dimples hugged her back. "Girlfriend, I'm moving on. I know when it's time to make an exit. The truth is, Ike don't look at me the way he looks at you. Girl, there are many more fish in the sea, and I've never been lonely or without a man's company or attention."

"Dimples, are you sure?" Serena's eyes were filled with compassion and curiosity.

"I'm very sure," Dimples smiled. "Serena, you don't even have to set a trap, scheme, or connive to get Ike. You better go get that man before he pops a gasket. He needs a woman like quick, fast, and in a hurry."

The back door opened with Sam and Gladys entrance. Serena and Dimples instantly changed the conversation. From all indication, they both felt a sense of relief in the matter of Cecil Isaac Webb.

The next day, Ike and Dimples sat across from each other having a similar conversation over lunch. He could no longer avoid the fact that Dimples was possibly pursuing him and that her interests were more than just platonic.  He'd been out of the dating game for a few months, but he still knew how to play the game.

"Dimples, I think it's time for us to seriously talk about our friendship," Ike stated over his salad.

He wasn't sure if this was the right approach. Or, if they should be having this conversation in a public place. He didn't want an emotional scene with Dimples.

"Is this the reason for our lunch date?" Dimples responded curtly. "You want me, to advise you, on how to handle my obvious interest in you, while you have eyes for my best friend, Serena? Ike, is that the topic of discussion?"

It startled Ike that she had stated so clearly the matter to be discussed. The lunch date was suddenly getting a little tensed. Ike glanced around the small courtyard restaurant to see who would be witnessing this headed for disaster meeting with his coworker and church member.

"Basically....," he replied. "Look Dimples, I knew this wasn't going to be a comfortable conversation but it needs to happen. We need to be honest and fair with each other. Just tell me if I'm wrong about this?"

"Wrong about what?" Dimples replied smugly. "Wrong that I have admired you since I first met you? Wrong that I've tried to get you interested in me? Wrong about me seeing a good man and hoping that he would feel about me the way I feel about him? I know you expect me to act all calm about this, but I'm not. Okay, honest, and fair with each other I'm going to be. You'll get my full emotions, now that you've asked."

She was being very direct and firm, while keeping her voice at a low moderate tone.

"Dimples," Ike replied softly, looking her directly in the eye. "I just want to do the right thing. All of my life I've screwed around with women's minds, bodies, and emotions. There was a time that I didn't think twice about anybody's feelings but my own. I got my cake, pie, and ice cream. It didn't matter who got hurt in the process. I'm not going to lie and say I don't have feelings for Serena. Because I have since I first laid eyes on her. I also have feelings of mutual respect and concern for you and our friendship. You've been here for me since day one and I thank you for it. Your friendship got me through some lonely and rough days. I doubt if I would've ever found the Lord, if it hadn't been for you leading me to your church. I'm sorry if I've misled you in anyway about our friendship. I'm begging you to please accept my apology and to forgive me?"

Dimple's heart softened. Ike hadn't misled her in any way. He had been true as a boy scout on every turn.

"Ike, I'm the one who should be apologizing," she replied. "Here I am trying to sweat you about something that you've handle right since the beginning. I was the one trying to hook and crook you any way that I could. Talk about screwing up relationships. You can call me the queen. Ike, can you forgive me for hoping that we could become something more than you want or feel for me?"

"Yes, by all means I forgive you," Ike sighed. "I just need to know I have your forgiveness for becoming so dependent on you at work. Dimples, you're one of my best friends, and I sure don't want to lose your friendship. But, you had to have known that I'm interested in Serena."

"It's okay, Ike, I know your heart is with Serena. I would have to be blind to have not seen it. Your biggest challenge is getting Serena to be honest about her feelings. She's pretty stubborn and has her own way of handling matters of the heart. So if you want my advice, then you need to handle her with kid gloves. You never know which way she's going to take."

Ike took in Dimple's words with much appreciation and thought. He was just thankful that their conversation didn't take a wrong turn and end up being a disaster.

"Thanks for the advice on handling Serena," Ike reached over and touched Dimple's hand. "See, I'm going to put God's word on her. Serena and I are very similar. We're both looking for divine intervention in our lives. I know I've made a u-turn and she's doing the same. Believe me, I know how to handle Serena Garrett."

"Well, I guess I've not come to that crossroad yet," Dimples sighed. "I guess I'm what they call still straddling the fence. Ike, don't get me wrong, because I truly love the Lord, and the church, and I know he is a forgiving God. I'm praying every day that I soon come into a full life in him. But, right now, I'm having too much fun out here."

"Dimples, I'm not going to sit here and give you a lecture because you know just as well as I do about the consequences of sin. But, I will be praying for your new change of mind and heart to happen soon, as in suddenly."

"Thanks Ike," Dimples smiled. "I do believe you've truly been changed. Like the song says, a wonderful change has come over you."

"True indeed," Ike responded softly. "And now I'm trying to live my life as a child of God and to walk this walk as upright as I know how."

Dimples took his hand in her hands and smiled happily across the table at her coworker, church member, and friend. "Ike, you're a good man and I'm proud to call you my friend."

One week later Clarice Webb walked into the place that she would call home for the next six months. Ike's condo was large and spacious. He gave her the master bedroom so that she would have all the privacy she needed. There was a sitting area with a television on one side  of the room and a master walk-in closet on the other side. She enjoyed the oversized Jacuzzi bathtub. The full-length wall mirror captured her image from various angles.

"Not bad for a fifty-six year old golden girl," she smiled. "Maybe, this pacemaker is going to add some more years to my life. I'm going to help it by finding all the beauty and age defying tricks on the market. Like my girl Patti says, *I got a new attitude.*"

Ike's bedroom was down the hall and across from a smaller bedroom that he utilized as an office. Clarice peeped into his bedroom and admired its order. Aside from an oversized chair with a few discarded clothing and a gym bag, everything else was neat and orderly. He had a smaller bathroom with a walk in shower. His closet was organized with shirts and suits hanging properly with an apparent color-coding system. His dress shoes were neatly aligned across the top shelves. The dresser-top was filled with an assortment of colognes and two large African candlesticks. His African print comforter with oversized matching pillow shams accented the room's decor.

His office space had the same orderly appeal. Clarice observed the clutter-free desk with an open Bible. She sat in the comfortable high-back leather office chair, and soaked in her son's orderly world. In one drawer there were files labeled budget and expenses, promotion opportunities, and personal development. In another set of drawers were files for Faith Baptist Church—men's ministry, outreach and evangelism, workshops and retreats. The bookcase was filled with an assortment of books on church growth, marriage and family, time management, and other subjects.

Clarice was beyond proud of Isaac. She was moved to tears just sitting there in his home office.

"Lord, how can I thank you," she wept silently. "Who would've ever thought that I could raise a son like Isaac. Lord, I thank you for my children. If it means never picking up a beer bottle or cigarettes again, I'll do it. And Lord, I know they want me in church and I'm almost there. Just be patient with me just a little longer. I hope that I don't backslide to my worldly ways. I got to make sure all of that is out of my system before I start promising you and everybody else. So, Lord, I thank you," she prayed softly.

"Hey Foxy! I'll be home in about twenty minutes. There's a soul food place around the corner. It's not too late for an evening snack."

Ike's cheerful voice was music to Clarice's ears. "You just come on home to my soul food kitchen," she fussed.

"Mama, you supposed to be resting."

"Boy, there is only so much rest I need. You got food in here that needed cooking. I got busy and cooked."

"We must be having microwave a la carte and protein energy supplements," Ike laughed loudly.

"You just come on home and see how resourceful I can be. I've worked with a little of nothing all of my life," she responded cheerfully. "Just do me a big favor and bring me something strong to drink."

"Now wait just a minute," Ike scowled. "Marlene told me that your diet is pretty much your decision. And, that there was to be absolutely no beer and cigarettes. So why you want to get here with me and change the rules?"

Clarice detected his irritation. "I'm talking about a Dr. Pepper or something like that. You know I like Root Beer and can sodas. That's about the only strong thing I've had since the heart attack."

"Okay, I misunderstood you," Ike apologized. "I want you healthy and alive."

"I'm going to be a good patient," Clarice laughed. "Also pick me up a deck of playing cards. I still like to play solitaire. I couldn't find a deck of cards around here nowhere."

"Sure thing Foxy. I'll even play a few games of spades with you," Ike responded cheerfully disconnecting the call.

Ike had requested a temporary schedule change to accommodate Clarice's first week with him. First shift was more ideal, but second shift had its set of advantages. More so, it was his attempt to defuse daily interactions with Dimples on a regular basis. After all, the less he saw of Dimples was the best solution for all of them.

Mack Earl Harper, the local drunk and homeless person, had become Ike's good buddy. The Mack Earls of the world were no stranger to him. It was men like Mack Earl that had inundated his childhood as the only father figures he had known.

Mack Earl was fifty-eight years old, tall, thin, and ruggedly handsome in an odd kind of way. A little cleaning up, fattening up, and a woman's touch could easily get him back in stride. For the last twenty years, Jack Daniel, and

Seagram's had become his all and all. He'd managed to work miscellaneous jobs to keep himself going, but mostly whatever woman was in his life at the time carried him.

Mack Earl had finally stopped going through the motions of joining Faith Baptist Church every week. He was re-baptized and dedicated his life to Christ. With the support of Pastor Kenton and his AA Sponsor, he was actively attending meetings and on the road to healing. He had a forty hour week job as an inventory warehouse clerk. His two-bedroom duplex was within walking distance to the church. The City's bus line ran right in front of his house as dependable transportation to and from work. His leisure time was filled with church, Bible study, and AA meetings.

On Saturday mornings, he spent his time working with Samuel Garrett at the church doing maintenance work. On Saturday evening, he would meet up with Ike to canvass the neighborhood, play basketball, and hang out in the community.

"Ike, thank you for taking up with me. You don't know how much it's meant to have you in my life."

"Hey man," Ike laughed, "I've been hanging around with guys like you all my life. I could be dead and in my grave, but it was men like you who taught me how to pick and choose my battles in these streets."

Mack Earl felt comfortable talking to Ike. There were parts of his past that he couldn't hold inside anymore.

"I wish I could have done that for my own son," Mack Earl stated sadly. "Mason was my son's name. He would be around your age if he was living. Mason was twelve years old when I left him in Chicago. I never married his mother. I left Chicago and came here to Memphis. I had a good job and lived a pretty decent life for a couple of years. I sent for him a couple of summers and was going to take him permanently until I lost that job. I never did find another job that paid like that one. A couple of years passed and he was about sixteen when his mother called me and said she couldn't do anything with him. He was in a gang and he wouldn't listen to nobody. I finally went up there to get him and it took me a week to find him. When I found him he cussed me out and called me everything but his daddy."

"So you washed your hands of him?" Ike inquired.

"Not exactly," Mack Earl continued to tell his story. "I stayed up there another couple of months because I had already lost my job back here in Memphis. I heard he was calling himself *Mack at Night*. He was the ringleader of some gang and was developing a pretty bad reputation for car theft and selling drugs. I figured he would end up in prison, sprung on crack, or dead. I also hoped that he would come to his senses and straighten up. He came to see me one night before I left Chicago. I tried to get him to come back with me and we'll both make a new start together. I think he really wanted to come, but he didn't know how to get out of the gang. He told me that when he decided to change he would look me up in Memphis."

Ike was glad that Mack Earl was telling his story and that he could be a listening ear. "Did he ever come here?"

Mack Earl took a deep breath and continued to talk. "Well, about five years later, I was over this lady's house and the headline news was about three bank robbers being shot down and killed here in Memphis. When they flashed the pictures of the bank robbers, I recognized Mason instantly. Even though he was sixteen when I saw him last, it was no doubt in my mind that I was looking at my son. The name they had for him wasn't his name though. I called his mother in Chicago and she said he held left about a month ago. He was living down this way. She said he was trying to get out of the gang and was on the run."

Ike's heart dropped. He had hoped that this story would've ended differently. Mack Earl kept talking.

"I couldn't rest until I found out if that was my son. I went to the City Morgue and nobody had claimed his body. I asked the other dead guy's family about his identity. A young woman knew that he came from Chicago and that they called him Mack at Night. She told me where he had been living and that he had some personal things there. She said that he was robbing the bank to buy his way out of the gang along with her brother. That was the only way they could get out of the gang."

Ike was all ears and Mack Earl stopped to wipe his tears. As he talked, the tears kept flowing. Something inside of him wouldn't let him stop talking. He needed to tell Ike the whole story.

"Who was this lady?" Ike's voice sounded hopeful. "Maybe, Mason talked to her. Maybe he told her something he didn't tell anyone else?"

Mack Earl took a deep sigh and continued his story. "The young lady told me that her brother was killed instantly, but that Mason lived about an hour after the shooting. One of the policeman said that Mason had asked for prayer. When I went with her to get his personal items, I found a picture of me, him, and his Mama. It was taken the day I left for Memphis when he was twelve years old. I claimed his body and buried him here. His Mama didn't even come for the graveside funeral. It was just me and the undertaker. There was no church service, no eulogy, no nothing. I wanted to say a few words but there was nothing to say.

"Man, that's a lot to go through. You have my deepest sympathy for the loss of your son," Ike stated. "I had no idea you had been through all of this."

"Nobody does," Mack Earl replied. "That's why I started drinking. That was all I could do to drown out the thought of my own flesh and blood coming to a no good end. He was here in Memphis and living right under my nose. I might as well have taken the gun and killed him myself because I didn't do right by my own son. He didn't have a chance in life. I failed him."

Ike had listened to Mack Earl with his heart. Mack Earl's deep sobs filled the small duplex on that Saturday afternoon. After a lengthy silence, Ike comforted his church member and friend the best he knew how.

"Mack Earl, it's a good thing that you've allowed yourself to let these memories surface. That is a hard thing to live with. God will forgive you, and he has forgiven you, but Mack you've got to forgive yourself."

"I know," Mack Earl sobbed. "I try and I'll do good for a while, but then the guilt and pain swells up in me, and won't nothing help but liquor. I believe he was going to find me after he did that bank robbery."

"Well, this time it's going to stick. You're going to stay on the wagon," Ike's voice was filled with hope and comfort. "Man, hang on to that and believe that Mason was coming back to you. Didn't you say he asked for prayer? That's hope and it says there was something in his heart that signified a change. God has given you a reason to hope and believe that his soul was saved. God has even changed you. Can't you see it?"

"How can you be so sure?" Mack Earl asked wiping his tears. "I've tried to change, but I've let so many people down through the years, including myself."

"I doubt that Mr. Harper. If God can change a pretty boy, smooth talking hustler, like me, then I know he can change you. I'm your Mason. If you ever wanted to do right by him then use me as your inspiration. My father died before I could get to know him. I was a grown man by the time he sobered up. When he sent for me he was already on his deathbed. Be my father! Do right by me! Don't let me lose you to alcoholism, too."

"Ike, do you really think Mason's soul was saved?" Mack Earl asked feeling hopeful.

"Only God knows that but I believe that since Mason had enough life left in him to ask for prayer, that he also asked God for forgiveness. And that fact gives me hope to believe that Mason was forgiven. Only you can believe that God left you this hope concerning Mason's soul."

Mack Earl found comfort in Ike's words. From that day forward Ike and Mack Earl's bond was solid. Mack Earl had a new inspiration for living. He felt that God had given him another chance to live and love again.

The following week, Ike and Pastor Kenton accompanied Mack Earl to the marked grave that had no headstone. The three men placed a headstone on Mason's grave. He was finally able to say a few words over his son.

"Thank you Lord for forgiving me of my sins. Thank you Lord for enabling me to forgive myself. Thank you Lord for my son's life. His life will forever be a symbol of hope and salvation in my life. Thank you Lord for letting Mason head this way some twenty years ago. We don't know, and we will never know what was in his heart. But, because he asked for prayer in his last hour, I believe that his soul is saved. This hope will live in my heart forever. This is my prayer. Amen."

After that, Mack Earl and Ike grew closer. The church community soon grew accustomed to seeing Ike and Mack Earl canvassing the surrounding neighborhoods. On Friday nights, the two men spent their outreach time talking with the teens and older men in the community. They gathered in an open courtyard behind the church to shoot basketball.

Afterwards, they would rest and talk under the shade tree. Their best conversations and biblical teachings happened during those times. Pastor Kenton had baptized seven men as a result of Ike and Mack Earl's shade tree evangelism.

Clarice celebrated her two month stay in Memphis by getting baptized. Faith Baptist had become a big part of her life. She looked forward to attending the senior's noon Bible study class on Tuesdays and  mid-week service on Wednesday nights. She really enjoyed working with the hospitality team in the fellowship hall on Sundays. And, she was becoming one of the most popular cooks in the church.

Clarice and Mack Earl met in the new member's class. She later started talking with him over the telephone when he would call for Ike. If Ike was asleep or not at home they would talk. Clarice felt comfortable with Mack Earl. Most of the men she had dated were from similar lifestyles as his. They were somebody's estranged husband, ex-husband, ex-convicts, deadbeat dads, hustlers, and gamblers. She knew his type well and identified with his struggle. It fascinated her that his change came through the church.

Mack Earl's attraction to Clarice was immediate. Right off he knew she was the kind of woman that he needed. The night he gave his testimony in new member's class, he felt as if he was speaking only to her. She was right there with him. Word for word she knew his testimony as if she'd heard it or lived it. Afterwards, she'd come up to him and introduced herself as Ike's mother. He left out of there floating. *"Lord, is this a new hope? I hope that there is a woman out here who can love me just the way I am. Please Lord, let this be a woman that I can call my own."*

Clarice felt an attraction to Mack Earl also. She was quick to recognize that he just needed a woman, like her, to bring him out. Staying in Memphis permanently wouldn't be too bad if their friendship continued.

"Well Lord, just maybe, there is hope for me," Clarice stated in prayer. *"I sure thank you for letting me meet someone like Mack Earl. He's an inspiration to a wretched soul as me."*

Serena and Pastor Kenton were having some serious struggles in getting the whole congregation to understand the church's role in the South Memphis community. Several grants were in motion with Faith Baptist being the  designated agency. But, there was a small group in the church that was set on causing conflict and confusion.

Instead of Wednesday's night mid-week service, a church meeting took place with city officials to address all questions and concerns about available grants and community development.

Pastor Kenton opened the meeting. "Church, this is a good purpose for us to gather tonight. We've been accepting the decline of this neighborhood and showing no concern as Christians. It's time for the church to take its rightful place in this community. This forum will open the floor for anyone to express their support or opposition. Now is the time to speak or forever hold your peace. We've gained the City's support and financial backing to turn this community around. What a great opportunity for change!"

The moderate sized sanctuary was full. It was hard to tell where everyone stood on the church's involvement. No one really wanted to openly expose their position. Serena felt the need for people to express their personal positions so they could get to the root of the contention. She raised her hand to speak.

"Faith Baptist should have taken a positive position to this growing problem of drugs, gang violence, and abandoned properties a long time ago. I have lived right across the street most of my life, and we feel relatively safe. However, this street is still contained, but beyond this circle our community has deteriorated. And again, I'll publicly say that Faith Baptist hasn't been much of a resource or help in any capacity."

An older gentleman sitting in the rear gave a short unpleasant grunt. He got up and headed for the side door, taking his wife, and a few other members with him.

"Wait just a minute Brother Gray," Pastor Kenton stood and acknowledged his abrupt departure. "Why don't you tell us your concerns? Everyone here has a voice and we'll respect each other opinions. Please brother, tell us what's on your mind."

Brother Gray was the ringleader of confusion and keeping things the same. He peered over his thick bifocals knowing that his sudden departure would cause confusion. Eagerly, he went to the podium.

"Brother Pastor, we've had this meeting before. Time and time again we have expressed that this problem is bigger than any of us. If the police ain't policing folks, and the elected officials ain't doing what they supposed to be doing, how is a bunch of law abiding Christian folks gonna fight crime, drugs, and those hoodlums out there? It seems like y'all just setting us up for trouble and to live in fear. I think we should just keep our church a place for safe peaceful worshipping. Leave them folk out in the streets, and out in the world where they belong. Ain't nobody in this church in their right mind is going to take on this massive mess of hogwash and politics."

Pastor Kenton moved from the pulpit and closer to the audience ushering Brother Gray and his followers to the front pew. He observed the murmuring and whispering and prayed that God would give him the answers that he needed. His expression was grieved and stony as he looked out over the audience.

"I'm sure a lot of you disfavor or feel uncomfortable with our church combating gangs, drugs, and the ills that have plagued our society, but we're Jesus' church. We have a responsibility in this community to be a light and a beacon and to offer hope. Those who come forth to work in this ministry will have to have a true call for outreach and evangelism. This is a calling that's not for everyone, but it's a work that must be done. God is going to hold each one of us accountable for our works."

"Pastor, you speak the truth," Samuel Garrett sounded from his seat. "I've been a member of this church for over fifty years. I can say there was a time when we were full force in this community, but that was a different day and age. I have the same fears and concerns as everyone else. But, as Christians, we need to be about making disciples and being fishers of men. God is going to protect us."

"Thank you Serena and Brother Garrett for those positive words," Pastor Kenton nodded appreciatively. "Those of you who feel like our dear Brother Gray please don't be afraid to speak up. You have a right to your opinion but know that God's work will go forth. There is a remnant of us here in this church that will bring this ministry forth. In time, I pray each of you will see the purpose and the need for the church to evangelize, help the needy, and save the lost. If you don't feel this is your calling then you are free to leave, but go in peace. And, know that a good work is about to go forth. Our church will be a vessel for community faith based programs."

Brother Gray stood up and about ten other older adults stood up with him. "Well, y'all can try to go ahead, but I got some people standing with me that will take this to City Hall if needed. Some of them officials sitting up there got their hands in the money pot and they're trying to use the church to cover up their crookedness. And, if you don't be careful, you'll be taking money under the table. If you haven't already done so."

Brother Gray's remarks were hateful. He and his followers made quite a commotion leaving the building.

Ike was entering the sanctuary when the naysayers were leaving. It was a challenge to get there at the six o'clock hour but he had promised Serena that he would be there. She was very clear in the purpose of the meeting and the need for his attendance.

Ike came down the side aisle and sat on a pew close to the front. He had tuned out the ongoing discussion and was busy reviewing the handouts. He was pleasantly distracted by Serena's smile when she looked over at him. He then heard his name nominated as the main speaker for a city-wide community event. Samuel Garrett and Mack Earl had already moved and seconded the nomination before he could even think of objecting.

"Ike, I think you have the voice for this community," Pastor Kenton responded joyfully. "A newly converted disciple and professional man, who don't mind telling his testimony, is certainly what is needed for this event."

Ike stood up and observed the nods of approval from everyone. "Sir, I don't doubt that it is," Ike stammered. "I may need a little more training before I start trying to speak publicly on such a large forum. I'm too much of a rookie."

"That is pure nonsense," Sam's voice ranged through the sanctuary. "If you didn't do nothing but say what you said when you got baptized that message can touch an army of people. Plus, what you and Mack Earl do in the community on the weekends under that shade tree ain't nothing but evangelism. Those boys and men look forward to that time."

Ike's smile confirmed his answer. "Well, ain't no rocks going to be speaking for me," he said boldly. "Put my name down, I'll do it."

The meeting ended with a definite rollout plan. The City Council's office would be in touch with Pastor Kenton and Serena as the official administrators over the grants and budgeting for feeding, housing, and the local community center's outreach programs.

After the meeting, Ike and Serena went along with a group of members to Denny's. Ike was starving and wanted to hear all the details about Brother Gray and his group. Pastor Kenton stayed behind with Sam to lock up.

"I hope Gray and his naysayers move on and start their own church," Sam stated. "His negativity and narrow mindedness is just a hindrance and nuisance to anything that represents change for the good."

"You're right Sam but Gray's type will always be with us," Pastor Kenton remarked. "I'm just thankful that God has sent Ike our way. With more men like him coming forth, we'll see change happen soon and in our lifetime. God's got some big plans for Ike."

"You ain't telling me anything that I don't already know," Sam laughed. "Me and Gladys is just hoping that our request for him is topping the Lord's list first."

"Ain't we all," Pastor Kenton laughed. "It's been a while since I've performed a wedding. You think I need to dust off my ceremonial robe?"

"Man, you need to burn it and buy a new one. For this wedding, we're rolling out the red carpet. I'm praying for nothing but the best for my daughter and new son-in-law," Sam grinned.

After Denny's, Ike followed Serena home. She didn't object when he suggested it. He was hoping that they could talk about something other than the church. She  parked her Mercedes under the carport and got into his new Infiniti QX60 sports utility vehicle.

"This is nice," she smiled.

"Not as nice as your Mercedes," Ike laughed. "When are you going to take me for a ride in it?"

"We can trade," she laughed. "This car is brand new and there is nothing like the smell of a new car."

"Where do you want to go?" Ike asked.

"The riverfront," Serena smiled. "It's such a pretty night and I love anywhere there is water."

Ike put on one of his Luther Vandross cd's. He was determined to get something said if it took somebody else to say it for him. He had never been intimidated by setting the right mood and atmosphere for romance. And, tonight was going to be his night to make his first move.

Serena was feeling the music and she was definitely in the mood for some romance. His choice of music was suggestive of something. She certainly wasn't going to keep him from taking the lead. Things were looking promising. Maybe, before the night was over, they would at least get in their first kiss.

Suddenly, Ike's car was breaking and screeching to a sudden stop. Out of nowhere, a car had pulled out in front of him and swerved into a telephone poll. They were not hit, but they felt quite shaken up.

"Are you okay?" Ike inquired nervously.

"Yes, what happened?" Serena breathe rapidly.

"I don't know," he stated, while unbuckling his seat belt. "Call 911….I'll check on the other car."

Serena called 911 and reported the accident. She watched as Ike knocked on the car windows. Several other cars had stopped to assist.

A few minutes later she heard sirens coming down Union Avenue. Ike came back to the car and reported that the driver was injured badly. He also recognized the driver as someone who worked at FedEx.

"I feel like I should go with him to the hospital," Ike stated. "He shouldn't be alone."

"Sure Ike," Serena agreed. "We can stay."

"No Serena," he stated firmly. "You don't have to stay. Just drive yourself back home. I'm going to ride with him in the ambulance and stay until his family come. I just feel like it's what I'm supposed to do."

"Well, I'm not just going to leave you either," Serena insisted. "I'll follow the ambulance. I'm doing what I supposed to do when it comes to supporting you."

Ike smiled. She was genuinely concerned and very serious. "Wow, I see that you're a real trooper and willing to go the distance in just about any situation. I like that."

"I can say the same about you," she smiled. "And, I like that too."

"This turned out to be some date, didn't it?" Ike stated. "Guess it wasn't meant to be."

"Was this a date?" she asked curiously. "I thought it was just a ride in your new car. I'm sure there will be many more times for us to go on an outing to the riverfront but a date. I don't recall you asking me out on a real date."

Ike flashed his signature playa's smile. "Woman, consider this our pre-date. We got flashing lights, whistles, and sirens going off. It can't get no better than this when you're with Cecil Isaac Webb. Wait just one minute, did you just feel the earth move from under your feet?"

Serena could feel herself blushing. Just that quick she turned into a giggling schoolgirl. "Ike, you're a mess," she laughed. "Be the Good Samaritan....I got your back."

Summer had come and gone amidst everybody's busy lifestyles. The hot and humid temperatures were still unseasonably warm. Occasional rain clouds hovered and provided a few  cool breezes. However, the beautiful foliage of colorful trees and leaves falling announced fall's arrival.

Serena and Ike were like two passing ships because both of their schedules were unpredictable and hectic. Ike purposely put a little time and space between them. He wanted to be certain that he would be more than just a rebound interest. He would have to use a different game strategy with her. She had been in love and deeply involved with Edgar Dupree. He had learned from experience that love was always intense when you were stealing it. Getting over a relationship like that would take some time, and he was in to win. Serena was worth the wait.

Dimples accepted a position on the West Coast. Truth be told, she didn't trust herself to be around Ike. Playing fair for something that she wanted wasn't her style. She decided to set her mind on moving up in the company. Ike had given her a great work reference from his station, which helped her get the job in Los Angeles.

Serena hosted a girl's night out for her send off. She knew that Dimples couldn't be trusted to play fair, and she was glad to hear that she was moving. Amidst their teary goodbyes, they both knew it was the best move and decision for all of them.

The following Sunday, First Baptist celebrated its 39th anniversary with morning and evening services. A full course dinner was served in the fellowship hall for all the members and visitors. Around *7:00* things  were finally winding down. Serena and Ike were among the last to leave before Sam locked up. Ike walked her across the street and they sat on the patio swing to enjoy the night air.

"Is it just me or do you see something developing between Clarice and Mack Earl?" Serena asked casually.

"Yeah, I got that too," Ike answered. "Who would've ever thought that Mack Earl would clean up so well? And, don't let me get started about my own mother. God is awesome! Things just seems to be falling in place."

Ike was quite content just watching the sun as it began to set in the westward sky. However, Serena seemed a little anxious and restless.

"You're right. I just don't understand how some things have progressed so well with people who have just met. And, things with other people aren't moving at all."

Ike looked at her curiously. "That's interesting," he stated, feeling a smile coming on. "Who are these other people? You want to elaborate on that statement."

Serena was beginning to feel a little nervous. She couldn't understand why she and Ike hadn't gotten farther along in their friendship.

"Well, to be direct, it seems that everybody seems to think that you and I should be together. But, for some reason God hasn't given us the memo with instructions on how to get from point A to point B."

Ike couldn't contain his laughter any longer. Was she finally expressing some interest in getting it on with him?

"Yes he did," Ike laughed. "In the memo, which is the Bible, the topic is addressed thoroughly. I certainly know how to move from A to B. I'm just waiting on all the signals and lights to turn green."

Serena was amused. She was feeling very flirtatious. "What color are the lights now?" she asked, looking deep into his eyes, while crossing her legs, and letting her foot gently brush up against his leg.

Ike studied the softness of her face in the evening light. He liked everything about her including the small patch of freckles sprinkled across her pretty face. She wasn't quite just where he wanted her yet, but she was getting there. He would have to exercise caution.

"Yellow and green. I promise that you'll be the first to know when there is one solid color," he laughed.

"What happened to red?" she asked curiously.

"Should red be included?" he asked slowly.

"I think we passed red a long time ago."

Ike rested his arm on the back of the swing and pulled her close. She felt good and that was about as much as he could take. His prayer was that he could survive a commitment of abstinence. It was something he had never done before. It was going to be difficult but he was willing to stay the course.

"Serena, we're going to do this God's way," he whispered softly in her ear. "It's the best way for both of us. Get that out of your head that I don't know how to get from one point to the next. Soon as I get the green signal, you're going to feel the earth move from under your feet for real!"

His voice was deep and seductive. Serena could feel her heart melting. Ike stood and pulled her up from the swing and held her tight.

"God don't put no more on you than you can bear. I think it's time for us to say good night."

"Already! But, it's still so early."

"It's later than you think," he sighed heavily, pulling her into his full embrace and leaning in close to her face.

His kiss was tantalizing and sensuous. Their lips were hot and hungry for each other's kiss. He backed away and smiled. She watched him walk across the street to his car. He turned and waved goodbye. She whispered a prayer.

"Soon Lord, please let it be soon, for both our sakes."

The holiday spirit was everywhere. Thanksgiving Day was just a few days away. Department stores were already playing Christmas music. There were still a few sweater wearing days but overall the weather had turned cold.

Ike was on a three week station assignment in Anchorage, Alaska. He saw it as a great career move for his future in senior management. The assignment would have him home by Thanksgiving Day.

Clarice was anxiously awaiting her new assignment as head cook for the grant funded feeding program at the church. She would be responsible for menu planning and supervising two assistants on her staff. The program was funded for one year and provided one hot meal and a food pantry for community recipients. Clarice and her staff were compensated through the grant's budget.

"Time really does fly," Clarice laughed into the telephone. "Marlene, I've been here just five months and my whole life has changed. I'm still in shock that I'm going to actually be working and paid through a grant project."

"It's certainly been a change for the best," Marlene stated back. "Mom, I'm just sorry that we can't be there for Thanksgiving. I promised to be with the in-laws this year, but we'll be there for Christmas."

"Sure thing sweetheart. I can't wait to see y'all again," Clarice said, shifting the phone from one ear to the other, while stirring a hot pot on the stove. "I better hang up before this caramel sauce becomes candy apple sauce. I'm testing some new recipes that I found on the Internet. Sweetie, I love you and kiss my grands for me."

Soon as Clarice hung up the phone ranged again. It was Ike letting her know that his assignment had ended. He would be flying back on one of the cargo flights and would be home in the early morning hours. He was off

Thanksgiving Day and the day after. Clarice hung up and called Gladys to tell her the news.

"It's a go," Clarice informed Gladys. "My dinner party for Thanksgiving Day is on. Ike will be back in town. You make sure Serena don't make any other dinner plans."

"That will not be a problem," Gladys laughed. "She's hungry for more than just food. I've never seen two young folks who got the hots for each other play it so cool."

"Well, it's a new scene for me too. But I'm bound and determined to get them two married off before the end of this year. At this point, I'm ready to pull out my shotgun and make them do the dang thang. Maybe, if she got pregnant, they'd have to get married then."

Gladys laughed loudly. "Now, now Clarice, I don't think it will be that extreme. It's so refreshing to see Ike court my daughter the old-fashioned way. I sure am in a hurry for some grandbabies though."

Clarice's recipe called for one half cup of cooking Sherry. She poured in two cups. "Well, we'll all have a good Thanksgiving and enjoy a great meal prepared by an upcoming chef par excellence as myself."

"Good night Clarice. And, please substitute the cooking Sherry or leave it out. You'll have us all feeling a little tipsy."

"Good night, my friend. A little cooking Sherry will not tip over a fly. Anyway, it will have evaporated. It's the rum cake that's going to do us in."

Both ladies hung up the phone laughing. Clarice poured the remaining Sherry down the sink and took the empty bottle to the dumpster.

"No sense in getting Rev. Ike all bent out of shape," she whispered. "He'll blow a gasket if he even thinks I sniffed some rubbing alcohol. But, that's my boy and I love him."

On Thanksgiving day, Clarice's dinner party at Ike's condo was going down. Pastor Kenton and First Lady Marie, Sam and Gladys, Mack Earl, Ike and Serena, were the invited guest. The aroma of marinated smoked turkey, cooked in a special blend of seasonings from Clarice's recipe collection was the main entrée. Cornbread dressing, buttered asparagus, steamed squash with smothered onions, sweet potato casserole, chilled cranberry sauce, homemade yeast rolls, and cornbread muffins accompanied the dinner.

"Everything smells and taste scrumptious," Gladys remarked at the dining table.

Sam took a bite of turkey, "I don't think I've ever tasted turkey as juicy and tender as this in my life."

"The secret is in the blend of spices," Clarice smiled proudly. "A little ginger, cumin, soy sauce, and a few other select herbs and seasonings."

"These vegetables are steamed perfect," Serena added. "You're going to have to share the recipe?"

"It's a possibility," Clarice winked playful at Serena. "It has to be kept in the family that's the only catch."

Mack Earl's plate was already half gone before he was able to offer any comments about the meal. "Clarice, I can only imagine that every meal you prepare at the church is going to be a blessed feeding. I hoped you cooked enough because I'm going to have to get seconds and thirds."

Laughter filled the room. Clarice refilled the serving platters and tea glasses. Pastor Kenton finally pushed back from the table. "Well, I'm convinced that the feeding program is in good hands beyond what we ever imagined. Thank God for the culinary skills of Clarice Webb."

Just before Clarice served dessert, Ike presented a chilled non-alcoholic sparkling beverage. He went around the table and poured some into everyone's wine glass. He poured his last and offered a toast. Everyone lifted their glasses as he spoke proudly.

"Let's give a toast to my mother's culinary skills. She got some kind of talent y'all. I'm going to hire her out with chef-par-excellence ratings."

Clarice was beaming with satisfaction. "I admit I was going for something other than the traditional spread. So that's why I went on the Internet to see what royalty was eating these days," she chuckled.

Again, laughter filled the dining room as she served the dessert. She'd prepared a coffee flavored custard ice cream topped with a cream de cacao sauce. The tasty homemade ice cream was the talk of the table. Second servings were served with homemade pecan pie.

"What happened to the rum cake?" Gladys asked.

"It can't be served before it's time," Clarice laughed. "It'll be ready for Christmas."

"Sounds like it might be loaded," Mack Earl laughed, giving Clarice a quick wink.

"You are right about it," Clarice smiled. "Grown folk's cake that's all I got to say."

Ike shook his head. "I'll make sure the cake is taken to the nearest dry county as a Christmas gift."

The room filled with laughter. Everyone was having a good time and couldn't have found a better place to be on Thanksgiving Day.

A few hours later Pastor Kenton and First Lady Marie said their goodbyes. Mack Earl, Sam, and Gladys agreed that they should stay to help clean up. Clarice put them to work in the kitchen and insisted that Ike and Serena entertain themselves in the living room.

Ike muted the television set and turned on the CD player. Soft smooth contemporary jazz came from the surround sound speakers. Serena took a seat on the mahogany leather love seat. Ike came and sat next to her.

"You know there is a conspiracy working here to get us together," Serena laughed.

"Stevie Wonder and Ray Charles would both agree," Ike smiled, pulling her closer to him.

He enjoyed the closeness of her body and watching her eyes twinkle with laughter. He put his arm on the back of the sofa to draw her even closer to him. Leaning slightly against his chest, she could feel the beat of his heart underneath his cashmere sweater.

"How about we go see a movie?" he asked.

"Is this an escape plan?" Serena giggled.

"Yes," Ike gave her a gentle squeeze. "I fear that the walls here have suddenly developed eyes and ears."

Serena smiled in agreement. "You get our coats and I'll tell the matchmakers that we're leaving."

Ike stood up and pulled Serena into his arms. Without any hesitation their lips met. The kiss was gentle and passionate. Both of them were very aware of the intense intimate feelings going through their bodies. Ike pulled her closer and she surrendered fully into his embrace. The second kiss was long, slow, and intoxicating with neither wanting to let go of the other.

"I thought dessert had been served," he whispered.

"Obviously it wasn't enough," she stated softly.

"Serena, what we got is a fine wine. You can't serve it before its time," Ike stated, while taking in the fragrance of her perfume.

The kitchen was all ears. Clarice quietly peeked around the kitchen wall and reported back.

"Houston, we got lift off. They're in one hell of a lip lock," she squealed softly. "My money is on a Christmas wedding. Any takers?"

"Let the church say Amen!" Mack Earl grinned.

Serena exited from Ike's embrace, smiled, and walked away. She could still feel his mouth on hers and his arms pulling her closer and closer into his body. Glancing over her shoulder, he was standing there looking as happy and content as she was feeling.

"What color are the lights now?" she asked.

"Two solid green lights and one big yellow one," Ike grinned.

The movie cinema parking lot was full with holiday movie goers. As an alternate plan, they decided on a romantic horse and buggy ride around downtown Memphis. The night air was seasonally chilled but a light blanket with both of them snuggled together would keep things at a good temperature.

While driving downtown, Ike turned the volume up on the *FM* radio talk station. The topic for the real talk was *"Does Abstinence Exist Anymore?"* They both looked at each other curiously and listened attentively.

A woman was phoning in to say that it was possible and those who were abstaining were in a minority. Another caller felt that he needed to sample or test drive any product before buying it, especially before marriage. The next caller stated that only religious freaks practiced abstinence. And, they were quick to rush to the altar so that they could hurry up and get their sex on. The next caller stated that the birds and bees were doing it. So why did humans have to put rules and time parameters on human intercourse?

Serena reached over and turned off the radio. "Maybe, that's a sign that we should be having a real talk session of our own," she stated.

"Yeah, I was thinking about calling in," Ike laughed. Suddenly and without any warning the traffic light turned red. Ike had to hit the brakes abruptly.

"Wow, did you see how quick that light changed to red?" he asked curiously.

"It must have malfunctioned," Serena replied. "Feels kind of strange....almost like divine intervention."

"That's exactly how I'm taking it," Ike stated. "Let's go to your house and talk. We can do that horse and buggy ride on tomorrow night."

"I agree because we should be on one accord before going on a real talk radio show."

Ike glanced over at her curiously. "I thought that we were on one accord. Aren't we?"

The light changed to green and Ike drove off. They were both silent. They were both giving the question of abstinence some serious thoughts. When they sat on the couch at the Garrett's home, they were more than ready for some real talk.

"Am I really that off base for wanting or believing that we can have an abstinent dating relationship?" Ike asked.

"Well, aren't you being a bit presumptuous?" Serena replied. "Are we dating? Are we in a relationship? Am I your woman? Are you my man? Are we a couple?"

Ike's whole facial expression changed from confident to uncertainty. He'd been so consumed with the spiritual aspects of being with Serena, until he'd neglected to carry things out in the natural. He looked her square in the face.

"Damn straight, we're dating and you're my woman," he grinned. "Girl, didn't you get that memo from heaven? Not only are we dating but we're engaged too. I thought you knew it."

Serena's mouth curled into a big smile. "Ike, you're just making this up as you go along. Aren't you?" she laughed. "Who's writing your script?"

Ike moved closer to her. He was feeling a little ungrounded. "I see that you're going to make a brother get on his knees," he replied.

Serena sat back on the couch looking snug and serene. In one quick movement, Ike slid off the couch on bended knee. He took her hands into his and turned very serious.

"Serena, I'm asking you to be my girl, my lady, my woman, and I need you to be my wife. Will you marry me?"

Just like that it had happened. Ike's voice was confident and filled with emotion. Serena could see, feel, and hear the evidence of her answered prayers. She didn't know whether to laugh, cry, jump up and down, or faint. Ike was actually on bended knee asking her to marry him.

Their eyes locked together in one long embrace. It seemed like time stood still while he waited on her to speak.

"Ike, don't you think we need to know if we're sexually compatible before we get married?" she asked.

"Baby, I have no doubt about bombs bursting and lightning flashing when we get it on. A house built on sex will have a poor foundation, especially my house. I'm more concerned about us being equally yoked and establishing our marriage on God's word."

Serena's eyes were filled with tears. Everything inside of her was screaming YES! She couldn't believe that God was giving her a gift of a changed man as Cecil Isaac Webb. Ike was truly exemplifying sincerity in his spiritual walk and most of all in looking for a wife. He would truly be a husband that she could call her own. Again, time stood still while he waited on her to respond.

"Ike, I agree. Yes, sex has a way of clouding your judgment. Ecstasy and orgasms take the place of love and respect. I want that thing that will hold us together when we're old and sexual desires are non-existent. I want the kind of love that will keep us together forever."

"Me too," Ike smiled. "Baby, when we become ancient of days, the sizzling memories of our passionate lovemaking will warm our thoughts and aging bodies."

"Ike, why is this beginning to sound silly?" Serena laughed. "I'm being very serious."

"I am too," he laughed. "I'm aging as we speak while bending on this one knee."

Ike put both his knees on the floor and pulled her down to him in a kneeling position. Face to face and with one spirit they both desired to be of the same understanding and mindset.

"Serena, do we both agree and see that God's plan for us is to abstain from sex while dating, and focus on building our relationship and marriage on His word?"

Serena eyes filled with tears. "Yes Ike, I agree we should abstain from sex. And I do respect the course which God has mandated for us."

Ike could feel his own eyes misting with tears. "Serena, I don't think you and I are virgins in no way whatsoever in knowing how to please each other. Nor, is sex going to be the ultimate in our relationship. However, it will be our second ultimate. So, do you belong to me? Will you be my wife for life?"

"Yes Ike, I belong to you and I'll be your wife for life," she smiled with tears flowing.

Ike took her in his arms and held her tight. They held on to each other. Neither one of them wanted to let go. They were both rejoicing for their answered prayers.

At *3:00* the following afternoon, Ike and Serena went shopping for his and her engagement rings. After the ring shopping, they took a horse and buggy ride downtown and enjoyed the sights on Beale Street. They had decided to announce their engagement during Sunday evening dinner with their parents.

Sam, Gladys, Clarice, and Mack Earl were all very excited when Ike and Serena made their announcement just before dinner. Ike asked for Sam and Gladys permission to marry their daughter. After their excited responses, Ike officially placed the engagement ring on Serena's finger. Serena placed a ring on Ike's finger to symbolize their commitment to abstain from sexual intercourse until they were joined together in holy matrimony.

"Clarice said it was going to happen but I didn't think it would be this quick," Gladys exclaimed joyfully. "It's just beautiful how it's coming together. It seems almost divine. It feels like we've just witnessed something very sacred. I've never seen this before."

A tear rolled out one corner of Sam's eye and down his face. He embraced Ike and gave him a big pat on the back. Serena teared up just watching her father hug Ike with so much love.

"Ike, me and Gladys, will be proud to call you our son. You've made us some happy people on today. I don't have any doubt that you will take care of our daughter and treat her with the utmost love and respect."

Clarice eyes were filled with tears of joy. "I don't have a clue how these things usually roll out. I've always known that Serena was the girl for my Ike. I saw it the first day I met her in this room," Clarice boasted. "Yes, it's definitely divine from where I'm sitting."

"Me too," Mack Earl chimed in. "All y'all need now is the marriage license to hook up. I doubt if you two can make it through a long engagement. When is the big wedding date? I've got to make sure I have a tuxedo."

The room fell silent. Ike and Serena glanced at each other. "Ike's going to set the date," Serena stated. "He's the spiritual vessel that's receiving the messages and signals."

Everyone remained silent waiting for Ike to respond. "She's right," he laughed. "As a matter of fact, I got the answer in worship service today."

Serena's eyes lit up with excitement. "Really, what is the date?" she asked.

"In ninety days?" he stated firmly. "That's what came in my spirit during my devotional this morning. Then Pastor Kenton confirmed it when he said that in ninety days God's favor would come in like a flood."

Serena smiled. "Ninety days is perfect. I love it."

Ike came over and gave her a passionate kiss. Serena responded and gave back fully with all the excitement of being caught up in the moment.

"Ninety days is going to seem like nine years if y'all keep that up," Clarice stated. "You two trying to be abstinent is truly going to be divine if you ask me."

Everyone laughed including Ike and Serena. "Don't worry Mama, Serena and I are equipped to do this. It can be done!" Ike replied.

"Swear it on this Bible," Clarice laughed, while holding up one of Gladys' hardback novels. "Repeat after me, I promise to tell the truth, the whole truth, and nothing but the truth."

"Y'all gone need some super hero powers," Mack Earl laughed, shaking his head in disbelief.

Once again the small party of six exploded into laughter. They sounded like a church full of people at a joyous celebration.

Serena, Gladys, and Clarice were busy making wedding plans. Gladys had called the newspaper and submitted an engagement photo of the couple. She'd insisted that Serena give her names and addresses of out-of-town friends to send out engagement announcements. Serena insisted on keeping the wedding small and elegant.

Dimples accepted Serena's request to come home that weekend to be the maid of honor. Clarice was moved to tears when Ike asked Mack Earl to be his best man.

"Mama, I didn't know you were such a cry baby," Ike grinned. "Who else would be my best man? Mack and I are almost inseparable."

"Ike, you have a whole staff of guys your age that you could've asked, but you asked my man. It's just plum beautiful," she cried. "I hate I wasn't in place for Marlene when she got married. It was all because of my heathen ways and thinking at the time. She was forced to elope."

"Mama, don't do this to yourself," Ike responded. "Marlene can have a wedding if she really wants one. People remarry all the time."

"Ike I'm honored," Mack Earl stated, feeling a little choked up. "God has spoken. You've truly become my son."

"God wouldn't have had it any other way," Ike responded, giving Mack Earl a high five. "Mama, you taught me how to appreciate the Mack Earls in the world. Now that is something you did right. There is nothing pretentious about Foxy Fox or her children."

Mack Earl handed Clarice a roll of paper towel from Ike's kitchen counter. She was crying and laughing at the same time. Ike was truly surprised at her emotional state.

Mack Earl pulled up a chair and sat next to Clarice at the kitchen table. "Ike, what your mother is trying to tell you between those tears is that me and her got hitched last night. Yes sir, I got papers on this ol' Foxy Fox."

Ike's face froze. It seemed like time stood still. Mack Earl and Clarice looked and sounded far away as if they were in a tunnel.

"I just didn't know how to tell you," Clarice voice ranged out, regaining his attention. "Pastor Kenton married us in his office. I called Marlene afterwards and she was just as shocked as you are right now."

"Ike, are you okay? Do we have your blessings?" Mack Earl asked feeling anxious.

"Yes, of course," Ike gasped, catching his breath. "I just wasn't prepared to hear that. Wow, this is something! When did y'all hook up like that?"

"Boy, you can't see past Serena, the church, and your job," Clarice laughed. "But, we were pretty discreet."

"This was the best way for us," Mack Earl stated. "We didn't have any doubts about us getting hitched. We knew that it had to be quick and fast. No sense in two old timers like ourselves waiting around. Neither one of us was up to the sneaking around and shacking. We're in the church now and members of God's family."

The amazement on Ike's face was surreal. He'd never been so outdone in all of his life. Mack Earl held out Clarice's hand and showed off her wedding ring. Clarice was radiant. She was beaming with joy and pride.

"We didn't want to upstage you and Serena's wedding in any way," she smiled. "Pastor Kenton has been meeting with us for a few weeks with the counseling sessions. Y'all thought we were meeting about the feeding program. First Lady took some photographs and we'll have cake and ice cream after church service on Sunday. Marlene and her family are coming up for the celebration. I'll be moving into Mack's place on today. You'll be home alone and on your own again."

"Wow, all of this is making my head spin. I'm on board and ecstatic about it. Who would've ever guessed?" Ike sighed. "I got the perfect wedding gift. How about a cruise for the Christmas holidays? I'm not taking *NO* for an answer."

Mack Earl and Clarice mouths dropped open. Ike started dialing Corporate Travel on his cell phone. He immediately began talking to a travel agent acquiring dates and discount prices using his parental traveling benefits. Clarice had started crying again and Mack Earl was gently wiping away her tears and kissing her cheeks.

"See honey, I told you God had a plan for us too. You and I are in love and legal. You got a husband to call your own and I have a wife to call my own. We can't do nothing but prosper now," Mack Earl smiled.

Ike admired them from afar. He had a new stepfather and a new mother in mind and spirit. He couldn't wait to tell Serena so they could share in a family celebration. While on hold, his mind flashed back to his devotional thoughts and Pastor Kenton's confirmation.

"In ninety days God's favor will come in like a flood."

A reception for Mack Earl and Clarice was held at a small and cozy event place. The DJ's music was straight old school and everyone was having a good time. Mack Earl had acquired a karaoke system so that he could serenade his bride. He sung Eddie Floyd's *"I Never Found A Girl."*

Clarice was swept off her feet. Mack Earl had missed his life's calling. He was born to be an entertainer.

"Ain't no love, ain't no love, like my baby's love, It's like burnin' fire, all shut up in my bones. Ain't no lonely days, ain't no lonely lonely, lonely nights, Every little thing that she does I know the girl's alright.

'Cause I ain't never, never, found me a girl, to love me like you do, to love me like you do. Ain't no man, ain't no man, got a little woman like me. You got all the lovin' honey, what a sweet girl can claim.

You're every poor boys dream, and every rich man's prayer, but I don't need money, honey 'Cause you're always there. 'Cause I ain't never, never, found me a girl to love me like you do, to love me like you do. No I ain't never, never, found me a girl to love me like you do.

After Mack Earl finished his serenade, the original version went on repeat and everyone was invited to the dance floor. To Ike's surprise, he discovered that Serena couldn't dance. So for the rest of the evening, he and others, enjoyed teaching her how to cha-cha, two-step, and line dance. Clarice had all the moves and Mack Earl was a quick learner also. The atmosphere was electric and festive. Everyone was on the dance floor and having a good time. Sam took Gladys on the floor for a spin in the Hoveround.

Several times, Mack Earl and Serena danced together. "Mack Earl, I need to apologize to you," Serena stated. "I need to ask your forgiveness for being mean and hateful towards you in the past. You're a wonderful person. Can you forgive me?"

Mack Earl was almost moved to tears. "Serena, you and I both know that I was messed up. If it wasn't for y'all accepting me and keeping it real about my behavior, I doubt if I ever would've made a change. So you've helped me more that you've hurt me. Don't ever think anything different. You're one of the main people who inspired me to do better. So, no more talk about the past. We're cool."

Both of them felt a warm and genuine connection. By the end of the night they were dancing buddies.

Every time someone mentioned Ike and Serena's upcoming wedding, he grinned and she blushed. Serena could hardly believe that she would soon be standing before family and friends, with Ike, as husband and wife.

When the music changed to slow dancing, Ike danced with Serena and pulled her close.

"Are you happy?" he asked.

"I've never been happier," she smiled.

"I love you Serena Garrett," he whispered tenderly.

"I love you more Ike Webb," she whispered back.

Faith Baptist Youth Ministry had grown substantially through a few outreach efforts. The Neighborhood Watch Program that Samuel Garrett had coordinated proved to bring the community together more than expected. Pastor Kenton and Serena were  working with the City Council's office in submitting a new proposal to re-develop several boarded up houses, ten duplexes, an empty apartment building, and several empty buildings into a faith-based housing community.

Serena's schedule was like a revolving door. Her life had changed for the better. Edgar Dupree had become a faint memory. It was amazing how little she remembered about those years of being the other woman. Sometimes she felt as though she had amnesia. God had wiped her slate clean.

Christmas time was definitely in the air. Everyone was in the hustle and bustle of holiday shopping, cooking, and decorating. Clarice and Mack Earl rescheduled their honeymoon cruise to a spring date. They had been approved for a home in the newly developed housing project around the corner from the church. Participating in the government funded renovation of their home was top priority.

Gladys kept herself busy helping Serena with wedding plans. Sam was working overtime at the church setting up the stage for the Christmas drama, while staying busy with all the other church events. Serena studied for finals and managed the business of the church's grant programs with the City. She and Clarice had planned a special Community Christmas Dinner to kick off the new Food Justice programs.

Ike was working long holiday hours. On several Sundays, during peak season, he was back in the truck making deliveries to keep the packages moving. At the end of a shift, he was too exhausted to do anything but go home and pass out. He and Serena were like two passing ships and both were very grateful.

"Thank God for the telephone," Ike yawned. "It's about the only way we get to have any time together."

"It's divinely designed because the Lord knows what is best for both of us," Serena stated.

"Yeah right," Ike laughed. "I'm getting my share of cold showers."

"I agree," she laughed. "Sweetheart, get some sleep. I'll come by tomorrow after my finals. Pray that I get a passing grade because I've barely studied anything."

"Baby, you so smart, you could've been a schoolbook. You could've been anything that you wanted to be. And I can tell....the way you do the things you do."

"Goodnight Ike, you're tuning up with tunes from the 60's," Serena laughed.

"That's right. Girl, that's when music meant something. It could do the talking for you," Ike laughed.

After they hung up, Ike's phone ranged. He just knew it was Serena calling to talk some more because that was their pattern. She had beat him calling back this time. But, the voice on the other end wasn't Serena's voice.

"Hello Ike, I'm Evelyn Burgess. Do you remember me?"

"No, I don't," Ike replied.

"Come on Ike, think back about five years," she continued. "I was Debra's friend. Remember, she was dating your partner Greg. They hooked us up."

Ike's mind went back in time. "Yeah, I remember you now," he replied. "We went out a couple of times. It was nothing serious. We both knew the deal."

"You're right on the nothing serious. But, we did more than just went out. Do you remember that part?"

Ike tried to visualize her but there were just to many women in his past to zoom right in on her.

"Ike, you had quite the reputation of being a playa," she stated. "Just how many women have you slept with?"

Ike didn't respond. She was getting a little too personal. His mind was racing. He couldn't imagine why she would be calling him after all these years. How did she find him anyway? Most importantly, what did she want?

"What's this call about?" Ike asked abruptly. "I don't mean to sound rude but what do you want? Has something happened to Greg?"

"I don't know anything about Greg and Debra. I parted ways with them years ago."

"Well, what do you want?" Ike repeated. "And, how did you get my number anyway?"

"First of all, I work at FedEx in Atlanta and I saw you at an event at corporate headquarters. Secondly, as a station manager, your cell phone number is listed in the database. And last, but not least, you need to know that we made a child together, and I've finally decided to let you know."

Ike couldn't respond. He didn't know how to respond because his brain had stopped working. He sat on the edge of the bed and listened while the woman repeated herself several times and continued to talk.

"I know you probably have other children by other women, and I definitely didn't want to be one of your baby mamas. Believe me when I say that I had my reasons for not telling you. But, that has changed. You should know that you and I have a child together."

"Can you prove it's my child," Ike asked.

"Of course I'm prepared to prove she is your child. I'm not making any demands for child support. Or, to disrupt my life or your life. I simply owe it to my child to tell the truth. These things are very important as she gets older."

Ike could feel his ability to think returning. "Okay," he replied. "If she is my child then I want to know and do the right thing. We need to do a paternity test, right?"

"That's right," Evelyn agreed. "We can go on the Maury Povich television show too, if necessary. Ike, believe me when you see her, you'll know that you're her father. I've done what I needed to do."

Ike thought for a few minutes. "The sooner the better," he replied anxiously. "Just tell me what to do?"

"I live in Atlanta and we can come to Memphis. I've contacted a doctor for the test. We just need to set a date before the holidays. She has an opening on Wednesday of this week at *10:45am*. It'll take two weeks to get the results."

"Wednesday is good," Ike answered. "Just tell me where and I'll be there."

"We'll be driving back to Atlanta after the appointment. If you want to meet her, we can have breakfast at IHOP near Wolfchase."

"Does the child know what's going on?"

"Oh no! She doesn't remember my ex-husband. She has started asking about her daddy."

"Breakfast will be fine," Ike agreed. "You said this testing is on me. Are you saying that I'm paying the bill? It's okay if that's what you mean. I just need to know."

"Yes, that is exactly what I meant," Evelyn laughed. "You can afford it on a station manager's salary. If you're not maxed out paying child support already."

"That's not my method of operation. I was a playa not a fool. That's why I'm having difficulty understanding how did I trip up with you. If, indeed, this child is mine."

"I told you that I was on birth control but I lied. You had a condom and I convinced you not to use it. So you see,

I played you," she laughed. "And, you took me at my word. You didn't give it a second thought."

Ike decided to hold his comments. He had already said enough. "9:00am on Wednesday at IHOP. I'll be there."

"Lover boy, keep the date. I will go through the court system if I'm pushed," she stated, and hung up the phone.

Ike hung up the telephone. He didn't know how to feel. He didn't know whether to call Serena or to call his mother. He needed to talk to somebody. He didn't feel happy, sad, or angry. He just felt numb.

"Lord, I don't know who to talk to but you. Why is this happening now? Why is my past coming to me now in the form of a child? How many other women could be out there with this same claim? Lord, I'm so ashamed. What is Serena going to think? How will she respond to this? Help me Lord!"

At first appearances, Ike didn't know the woman waiving at him from a booth at IHOP. Her bleached blond hair and fuller figure, made it hard for him to recognize her. She was stunningly attractive and looked like the type he would've fooled around with. Sitting in front of her enabled him to have a flashback of those two dates. Yes indeed, he had known her and had slept with her.

It happened on a bet with Greg to see how long it would take for him to get into her panties. Ike had won the bet on the first date. He only took her out the second time because she was such an easy lay.

"Hello Evelyn. Yes, I do remember you."

"Do you really?" she laughed. "I've changed. I'm not as fine as I was five years ago. I'm finer with a little age."

"I do remember what is beneath all the weave, eyelashes, fingernails, makeup, and all the bling bling that you feel makes you beautiful."

"Ike, I'm going to take that as a compliment," she stated. "I see a few years has matured you also. You no longer look like a young ass hustler pimp wanna be gigolo."

Ike couldn't help but laugh out loud. She had tagged him right. Only someone from his past could truly label him for what his life was all about at that time.

"Where is the child?" he asked, after giving the waitress his order. "Isn't she why we're meeting?"

"I think we should talk a little more. She is with my sister and they will meet us at the doctor's office."

They spent the next few minutes eating their food. Ike was hungrier than he thought. Evelyn's phone was constantly ringing and she went to the ladies room. When she returned, Ike was ready to talk.

"Why would you keep this from me for five years?"

"Because, it was the best decision for me. I was married and separated when we met. I wanted to get back at my husband because he was sleeping around. I was surprised that you were so good looking and that made it even better. I went back to my husband after I slept with you the second time. A few weeks later, I was pregnant and I really didn't know whose child it was. He was so excited about the pregnancy. When I went into labor and gave birth, he was nowhere to be found. I was relieved because it gave me a chance to see the baby first. The minute that I laid my eyes on her I knew that she was yours. When my husband finally saw her, she melted his heart, and said she looked just like him. That's when I decided that you didn't need to know."

Ike was listening intently. "So why is it that I need to know now?" Ike asked calmly. "Is there more to this breaking news story than you're telling me?"

"Yes, it's about me needing to tell the truth. Also, I've divorced that piece of a man that I called a husband," she laughed. "He got women and children everywhere. Also, did you know that I am ten years older than you? Ike, you got a cougar pregnant."

Ike could feel a headache coming on. He couldn't get his head around all of the emotions going on inside of him. What did she want from him? Why was his past raising up now when his future was so on point? Parts of him was surprised, anxious, and skeptical. He hated the fact that he had been kept in the dark for five years. He hated that the child could be his and had been passed off as another man's child. If she was his daughter, he wanted to be a part of her life. How would Serena respond to this new development? Would he lose her love and respect?

"Listen Ike, I'm not doing this to mess up your life," Evelyn stated. "The longer I wait the more harm it will be for my daughter. I've made a good life for us in Atlanta. I got a man and I can take care of me and my daughter all by myself. When you accept that she is your child, you can share in the parental rights as you desire."

Ike listened but didn't respond. He just wanted to see the child. "What's her name?" he asked thoughtfully.

"I thought you would never ask. Her name is Ikayla Joy Burgess. Ikayla is a Hawaiian name. When I was visiting there I met a lady by that name. Also, it was my way of connecting your name to her in some sort of way. I call her Joy because she brings joy to my life."

"That's a sweet name," Ike replied. "Let's get this over with so the truth will be known."

His anticipation was becoming overwhelming. Deep in his heart, he felt that he was about to meet someone who was going to make a lifelong impression on him.

Five year old, Ikayla Joy Burgess was a bouncing bundle of joy. Ike's heart skipped a couple of beats when he looked into the eyes of the prettiest little girl he had ever seen. The likeness of him in her cute round innocent face was undeniable. He couldn't deny that he was looking at his flesh and blood. She was his seed. Evelyn could tell that he saw the resemblance.

"Didn't I tell you," she grinned. "If she was old enough to know, she would know too. She was about two years old when my husband asked me who was her daddy. By then, I was ready for him to leave. But, he wanted us to stay together in that sorry ass marriage. That's when I packed my bags, moved to Atlanta, and filed for a divorce. Joy and I have been on our own for three years now."

In the doctor's office, Ike sat next to Joy and watched her with excitement. Her hair was naturally curly and twisted in locks with a big pink and white bow on the side. She was dressed like a lovely doll in a pink and white ruffled dress, with matching socks, and white dress shoes. She was polite and very talkative.

"Are you going to see the doctor too?" she asked Ike. "Mommy says that we have to open our mouths wide to take a very important test."

"Yes, I'm going to take the test too," Ike smiled. "Are you afraid?"

She looked at Ike curiously. "If they stick me, will I get a sticker and a sucker?"

"I hope so," Ike laughed. For some reason, he sensed that there was much more to be seen of this little dolled up girl sitting next to him.

Evelyn was very curious as she watched Ike watching her child. "She has her Sunday best behavior going on right now. But, she can be quite a tomboy most of the time."

Ten minutes later, they both were being swabbed in the mouth for DNA. Ike had provided insurance information and his mailing address for the test results. A copy would be mailed to him and Evelyn in Atlanta.

He waited for them to return from the ladies room. Ikayla Joy had changed into her traveling clothes. She was wearing a pink and blue sweatshirt with a hoodie, pink and blue jeans, and white tennis shoes. She was still the most prettiest little girl he had ever seen. He watched as Evelyn put her in the car's booster seat and secured her seatbelt. They said their goodbyes.

"Bye Mr. Man," Ikayla Joy yelled from the window. "See you later alligator."

"After while crocodile," Ike yelled back.

He walked to his car in a daze. He could still hear her little voice saying Mr. Man. What was she supposed to call him? They didn't tell her his name. He had no doubt that he was her father. He was sure he would be disappointed if the test came back negative. This was a new experience, new feelings, and new emotions.

"Oh Lord," he sighed. "Ninety days your blessings will come in like a flood. What a blessing! I have a daughter. This is over the top!"

Ike rushed to his car and pulled out his cell phone. He couldn't wait to tell Serena all the details of his news.

"Lord, I thank you. But, I'm going need you to pave the way and make it right for Serena to accept this child into our lives. Lord, help us."

Ike's face was full of joy and apprehension as he told Serena his news. His life was an open book. Anything and everything that she wanted to know about his past was on the table for discussion. Serena realized that Ike's news could have been worse. It was  surprising, but not such a surprise that it would jeopardize their future.

"Ike, how can you be so sure before the tests come back?" Serena asked.

"I just know it," he sighed. "Baby, I felt like I was looking at a little mini-me. She looks like Marlene when she was that age. She looks like Marlene's daughter. I even see Clarice in her. It's amazing."

"Wow, you got some strong genes," Serena smiled. "So, you are a father after all."

Ike had prided himself on not having any children. He had always preceded the statement with "to my knowledge" when that subject came up.

"Serena, I never lied to you about my lifestyle. And, I seriously don't know if there are any other children out there. Yes, I used protection but there might have been a few more times when I didn't. I just don't know."

Serena had a few wandering thoughts. The words were forming in her mouth but she couldn't seem to articulate them. Just how many women had Ike been with? Surely there was a need for her to be concerned about health risks whenever they did consummate their marriage?

"What's on your mind?" Ike asked. "Come on baby, talk to me. We're adults and this is the time for real talk. Whatever you want to know just ask me. Now is the time."

"Ike, I think we both should have physicals and get tested for HIV and other sexually transmitted diseases. I haven't been a girl scout myself. Only God knows who Edgar Dupree slept with and I wasn't using any protection with him. The only smart thing that I did was to eat those birth control pills daily. I think that we owe it to ourselves to get checked out."

"Yes, you're right. When I went to work at FedEx, I was tested for everything under the sun. I can be tested again. You schedule the appointments and we can go together."

Serena sat quietly. "Real talk is depressing," she sighed heavily. "It ain't so pretty and serene."

"But, it's our reality," Ike stated. "Sin is ugly and disgusting. It kills, steals, and robs you of joy and dignity. It comes back and bite you. But, we've got to refuse to let it have any power over our lives and our future."

"Ike, we haven't talked about our own plans to have children," Serena stated. "We may not feel the same. I do want us to have children but not immediately. I want to finish school, become a counselor, and practice as a professional before motherhood."

Ike let her comments register for a minute. "That's fine. I just hope we're not talking too many years."

"Just a few," Serena smiled. "Plus, I've already gotten back on my birth control pills."

"Well that settles that," Ike replied. "Who am I to challenge the decisions you make concerning your body?"

"You will be my husband. Decisions concerning both of our bodies will be made together. But, now I'm on the pill."

Ike laughed. "For what? We ain't doing nothing."

"Let's change the subject," Serena smiled. "Did you take a picture of her? I would love to see her."

Ike shook his head. "No, we didn't. Evelyn wanted no pictures to be exchanged until after the test results."

"She's smart," Serena smiled. "A woman will use many tactics to prove and disapprove her theories. I pray she will be fair when it comes to you and our soon to be daughter."

All of Ike's worries and concerns dissolved when he heard those words. "Thank you my soon-to-be-wife-for-life.

I need you by my side in claiming this child. She's definitely my child. All I need is you and together we can conquer whatever comes against us."

"When are you going to tell our families that we have a little bun in the oven?" Serena laughed.

"The results will be back before Christmas Eve. It can be their Christmas presents. What do you think about that?"

"I think they will all stroke out," Serena laughed. "We can call her our immaculate conception. They will be overjoyed."

"I love you Serena Garrett," Ike whispered.

"I love you more Cecil Isaac Webb," she smiled.

"90 days," Ike laughed. "What more can happen?"

There was only two days left before Christmas Day. Faith Baptist Church was packed for the Christmas program and community fellowship. Mack Earl was suited up to be Santa Claus. Sam  managed the backstage area. Clarice and Gladys were busy with the other women preparing after show treats and Santa's gift bags. Serena was lending a helping hand with costumes and last minute speeches for the children. Ike was at work pulling double shifts to ensure his station was meeting customer demands.

In less than one year, First Baptist Church had a different rhythm and many new faces. The church was alive and thriving again. Pastor Kent was grateful and gave all the glory and praise to the Heavenly Father. In his closing remarks, his enthusiasm and words of thanks were heartfelt.

"A child was born and a King was given for the salvation of all who will only believe. Church, God is

moving and it's in our favor. So let us believe and have faith that God will sustain us as we move into a new year and new ministries. I hope and pray that everyone will have a joyous and happy holiday, and that the Lord will keep us in his loving care until we meet again. Let us all say together, Jesus is the reason for the season. Go in peace and be blessed!"

Christmas dinner was hosted at the renovated home of the newly married couple, Mr. and Mrs. Mack Earl Harper. Clarice had prepared a scrumptious holiday feast that satisfied everybody taste buds.

She had promised at the Thanksgiving dinner to save her signature Italian Cream Rum Cake for Christmas dinner. Ike had everyone cracking up when he warned them to eat at their own risk, and to put away all flammable objects, and to locate the nearest fire extinguishers and exits. Because that cake was qualified as a lethal weapon, loaded with liquor, and it was a bomb.

Clarice quickly shut him down. She gave him a slice of pound cake. Ike pushed his slice of cake away and begged until she gave him an oversized chunk of her specialty holiday cake. Again, everyone laughed until they cried.

After dinner they sat in the living room to talk about the renovated house and to open gifts.

"They've done an outstanding job on remodeling all these old houses," Sam stated.

Gladys agreed. "I like that y'all decided to keep the original framework. There is just something special about old houses with high ceilings and wraparound porches. To me, it has always signified romance and elegance."

Serena had been busy admiring the mahogany crown moulding, doors, windows, the trimming in the woodwork, and hardwood flooring in each room.

"Yes, this is definitely a Victorian Antebellum home. This was uptown southern living at its best years ago."

"Yeah, that's what I told Clarice," Mack Earl replied. "This street and all the way down to the other end of McLemore and Walker is where the affluent and uppity Negroes used to live."

Clarice was so proud of their home. She took in every compliment with joy and pride.

"Looking at the City's realty sheet, I thought a two-bedroom house was going to be too small for us, but these rooms are large. Plus, that room on the back is good for another bedroom or play room for the grandchildren."

"Speaking of grandchildren," Ike stated casually, "when will Marlene be coming?"

"They're coming next week and staying until after the new year for about two weeks," Clarice answered. "I'm sensing that all is not well at her house. Just don't say anything to her about my suspicions. I want her to tell me what's going on. You know how Marlene can be."

"Alright," Ike replied. "She'll let us know in her own time. It'll be a treat to have my big sister here with us for a while. Let's open these gifts."

Everyone opened and admired their various gifts. Ike and Serena had purchased matching fur-lined, brown leather vintage bomber jackets for themselves. The Harpers received an assortment of accessories for their home from everyone. Gladys and Sam received a Keurig coffee brewer with an assortment of coffees from Ike and Serena. Ike and Serena received two original oil paintings for their home from both sets of parents.

"Well, we have another gift," Ike announced, while Serena handed each couple a gift box.

"Just open it and don't say anything," Serena stated firmly. "I repeat, do not say a word."

Ike and Serena anxiously anticipated their reactions. Inside each box was an 8x10 glossy of Ikayla Joy. Each of the couples looked at their picture in silence. After a few seconds, Clarice gasped and put her hand over her mouth, while her eyes quickly filled with tears. Gladys looked up at Ike and smiled with misty eyes. Sam and Mack Earl had guessed it also.

"Merry Christmas," Ike stated, taking Serena's hand. "Her name is Ikayla Joy Burgess. I'm her father and she's my daughter. And, that makes y'all her grandparents."

"Ike, when did you find out?" What happened?" Clarice asked through tears of joy. "How old is she? Where is she?"

"Calm down Mama," Ike smiled. "I'm going to tell y'all the whole story. Just breathe for a few minutes."

"Serena, are you okay? How are you taking this?" Clarice asked anxiously.

"I'm fine," Serena smiled through teary eyes. "Ike's happy and I'm happy. God has given us a beautiful five year old daughter."

"That's right baby, accept her into your heart," Gladys chimed in lovingly. "Oh, she is so precious and beautiful. I love her already."

"Look at God," Sam shouted loudly, as he jumped up out of his seat.

Mack Earl was truly amazed. He sounded like the Holy Ghost had struck him too.

"Ike, man, this is some kind of a blessing. I ain't never in my life seen nothing come together like this. It looks like you done skipped over all that baby daddy and baby mama crap. I see you handling your business like grown folks supposed too. Boy, I'm so proud of you. Son, always do the right thing and right will always follow you!"

Ike and Serena couldn't stop smiling. "I told you that they were going to stroke out," Serena laughed.

"I had no idea," Ike laughed, holding Serena close. "Look, can y'all just chill. Y'all haven't given me a chance to tell you anything. Y'all don't even know the dynamics about the situation. I'm all ready to share and spill my guts. But, y'all just done knocked it out the park with love, nothing but love. Y'all some beautiful folks and I love y'all."

Sam had taken out his handkerchief to dry his tears. "What more do we need to know? A picture is worth a thousand words. You just said that you are the child's father. Spare us the details because that is you and Serena's business. We just want to see our grandchild in the flesh. When will that happy occasion happen?"

Gladys and Serena looked at each other and smiled. It was obvious that Sam was just as excited as Clarice. Serena blew her mother a kiss.

"Wait just one minute," Clarice stated. "Sam, you might not want to know, but I want to know all the dynamics. I want to know book, chapter, and verse. For sure, I want to know who is this heffa that kept this child from my son for five long years? That heffa gonna hear from me!"

"Ooops there it is," Mack Earl laughed. "That's what I'm talking about. That's my woman. Now, calm down baby....breathe....Ike got it. Let him handle his business."

Serena had gone into the kitchen and came back out with a tray filled with slices of honey baked ham, pound cake, and sweet potato pie. Mack Earl dashed into the kitchen and returned with egg nog, cold ginger ale, and bottled water. They all ate and admired Ikayla Joy's photo again. Each one told what they were going to do with the grandbaby. They were laughing and coming up with cute grandparent's names for each other.

Ike and Serena snuggled together on the couch and watched their parents.

"It makes you wonder how are they going to carry on when we have our child?" Ike smiled.

"I'm wondering how are they going to act at the wedding?" Serena smiled.

"Ninety days," Ike smirked. "What was I thinking? Lord, give me strength."

"Sixty days and counting down," Serena sighed. "My prayer is that the Lord gives us a special kind of strength that surpasses all understanding."

The new year came in with a bang for everyone. Snow and ice paralyzed the city. Schools and businesses were closed due to inclement weather. Marlene was visiting and had extended her holiday stay for an indefinite period of time. She was extremely pleased with Clarice's new lifestyle and her new step-father. Coming to Memphis had been good for her and the children. Ike's new family and his church family were a pleasant escape for them.

"Why don't you just tell me what is really going on?" Clarice pleaded with her daughter. "There ain't nothing you can tell me about your situation that will surprise me. Girl, come on and talk to me. I'll just listen. Trust me to that, ok?"

"It's not that Mom, it's just hard for me to say it. I just can't bring myself to believe it. I've turned a blind eye to my situation for too long. I can't deny it any longer."

Clarice was listening with all that she had inside of her. Ike had tried to find out what was going on with Marlene, but she wouldn't tell him either.

Clarice decided that she was going to get to the bottom of this thing. Even if meant cursing and getting Marlene mad and pissed off at her.

"Marlene, your husband has not called since you've been here. You don't say his name or nothing about him. The children don't even say nothing about him. Don't make me go into my old ways to get you to talk to me. So, please, talk to me. We need to know and we want to help because we love you and we're family."

Marlene stared out the window while holding a warm mug filled with hot chocolate. The sound of the children laughing in the other room with Mack Earl was refreshing. Sitting at the table with Clarice being sober, not cussing, and not talking about other folk's business was surreal. Suddenly, the tears just started flowing freely down her face. She looked at Clarice and broke down. Clarice knew her daughter well enough to not do anything to comfort her. She sat quietly and waited for her to cry it out.

"Mom, he isn't the man he made me believe that he was," she stated, between sobs. "He fooled me and his whole family. He has lied to all of us for years. I heard the rumors about him before we eloped. I didn't believe them because he was having sex with me and I got pregnant. I knew they were just lies. He told me they were lies. His mother told me they were lies. His daddy told me they were just lies. We all believed that they were just lies."

Clarice's gut told her what it was. She took a deep breath and spoke very softly. "I got it....he's been living with you while being on the down-low."

Marlene dried her eyes and stopped crying. She looked Clarice in the eye. "Yes Mom, that's my ugly truth!

For a few minutes they both sat in silence. Clarice processed her daughter's truth in her mind. She hated that this had happened to Marlene.

"It doesn't surprise me," Clarice sighed. "Now I understand why he never wanted to be around me. I would've read him like a book. I see it now."

Marlene words begin to flow freely. "About two years ago, he really started changing. I thought he was having an affair. He started coming home later and later. Then he stayed home all the time. When he was home he was depressed. We were still going to church and pretending to be this happy family. He lost his job and we went to counseling. He became suicidal. That's when his sisters and brothers got involved. Then his parents got involved. He left me a note and disappeared. His parents helped with the children and paid our bills. I just kept going to church and to work. The whole church was praying for us."

Clarice sat and listened. It wasn't time for her to say anything. Marlene kept talking.

"Mom, I didn't want to tell you and Ike. Y'all had new lives and I was just praying that my situation would turn around. Then he came home and told me that he wanted to be free. He said that he wasn't gay but that he was bi-sexual. He was involved with men and women. He liked both sexes. He told me to go and get myself tested for AIDS. He was moving to New York where he could live his life openly. So, that is my reality.....this is what I've been living."

Clarice didn't say a word. She got up from the kitchen table and took Marlene by the hand. She led her into her bedroom and closed the door.

"Come on shuga baby, get in this bed, and let your Mama hold you," Clarice stated, with tears trickling down her face. "I need to hold you. You got the love of your family and God's family. You can and will survive this."

Marlene laid her head on her mother's chest and cried. Clarice stroked her hair and rocked her softly. "Marlene, cry until you can' t cry no more. Everything is gonna be alright.

God got you. We got you. Weeping may endure for the night, but joy cometh in the morning."

Clarice hummed softly one of her favorite new hymns. *"Blessed assurance Jesus is mine......this is my story....this is my song....praising my Savior all the day long."*

Marlene's life was looking and feeling whole again. But, deep down on the inside, she felt that she would never be the same. She decided to make Memphis her home. She wanted and needed to be with her family. Her medical tests had come back negative. Other than being anemic and underweight, she was doing well. She and the children were seeing a Christian counselor to help them deal with their new found realities.

Ike was very instrumental in getting Marlene a job in the Call Center. Her in-laws were financing her until she could get on her feet. The children were enrolled in a charter school that Serena had found. Their new apartment was in the area where Ike lived. They joined Faith Baptist and quickly got involved in the life of the church. Clarice had become a doting mother and proud grandmother. She and Mack Earl were in parents and grandparents' heaven.

"Mom, I've always loved you," Marlene stated to Clarice lovingly. "I know that I've not shown it very much through the years. Can you ever forgive me?"

"Forgive you! Can you forgive me?" Clarice stated, feeling herself tearing up. "I'm the one who was foolish and irresponsible all of those years, and I'm the momma."

"And a very good mother, who did a good job in loving, providing, and taking care of us. I've learned so much from you all of my life. I'm so grateful that you are my mother."

For the first time, in a long time, Clarice was shocked and didn't know what to say. Marlene hugged her tight and Clarice held her even tighter.

"I'll see you and Pops tonight at my place," Marlene smiled. "I can't wait for you to see how I'm learning to out cook you. And, please be on time."

"Go on lil' girl," Clarice smiled. "The proof is in the pudding. I'll bring something just in case. You got to get up early to out cook this Foxy Fox."

Everyone was anxiously counting down the days until Ike and Serena's wedding. Appointments with cake bakers, caterers, wedding gown fittings, bridal registries, and all the hoopla that went along with wedding planning were in the works.

Serena was thankful that Gladys and Clarice were her wedding planners. Most of her time was spent studying and writing her thesis paper. Ike was doing a good job setting the tone for their abstinent relationship. He was actually enjoying their courtship and the waiting.

"Ike, what song are you humming?" Serena inquired curiously, looking up from her laptop. "You've been humming it quite a lot lately."

Ike was working on a life application teaching lesson that had been pressing on his heart.

"It's one of my theme songs," Ike grinned. "It reassures me that what we're doing is going to pay off. It's something that I'm looking forward too. It's keep me grounded."

Serena looked puzzled. "It doesn't sound like any spiritual tune that I've heard."

Ike kept his grin on his face. "Baby, it's a Freddy Jackson song. And you know, he was a choir boy. It's one of those back in the day tunes that Clarice used to play."

"Well, sing it. Let me hear it."

"Baby, its grown folk's music. It will put you in the zone of no return."

"So why are you singing it then?"

"It's Ike-ology. It's my strength when my flesh is weak. It sustains me with patience and longsuffering. It assures me that I'm going to win and get the prize at the end."

"Ike, you're sounding like a preacher," Serena stated, still looking puzzled. "I need to hear the lyrics so I can relate to the song's meaning."

"Patience, my dear, patience," Ike grinned. "You just keep writing that paper. I got something that I'm working on too."

For the next hour, they both focused on their work. A few minutes before midnight, Ike prepared to leave.

"It's getting late," he whispered, while pulling Serena in his arms. "I got a busy schedule on tomorrow and a men's fellowship outing."

"I know," Serena yawned, snuggling closer. "You and your 90 days did this to us."

"I know," Ike smiled. "You got to admit that it's a perfect arrangement for us."

"If you say so," Serena sighed.

"Absolutely! It's divinely designed for our good. God is doing something with this and He's using us to show that it's possible and doable."

"Yeah, right," she smiled. "Come on and give me my once a week, lukewarm, lover boy kiss, that has to last us until next Friday night."

"Girl, don't make me bring out the oil. You need much prayer," Ike laughed, while pressing his lips close to her ear. He pulled her tighter into his embrace and sung his song.

"Darlin' I, I could use a 'lil love right now. Whenever we touch like this, whenever I kiss your lips, baby my heart beats faster by the minute. Whenever I touch your face, you know I want you right here. I want you right now, cause there's so much pleasure in your embrace. Darlin' I, I could use a 'lil love right now. Darlin' I, I could use a 'lil love right now."

Serena's heart was melting softly while listening to his seductive tone and sexy lyrics. Ike was turning on every button in her thoughts and body.

"Baby, I'm all man and I don't want nobody but you," he whispered, kissing her passionately.

"Oh my goodness, 38 days and counting," she sighed, while slowly pushing him away from her.

Ike stepped away willingly. He put on his warm leather bomber jacket, fur-lined gloves, and his brown and beige plaid Elmer Fudd fur-lined hat with hanging ear flaps.

"That hat is awful," Serena laughed.

"Yeah, but this jacket, that my soon-to-be-wife gave me is banging," Ike winked. "Plus, Daddy Sam gave me this hat and I got to wear it."

"And you should've given it right back to him."

Both of their eyes were filled with love as they stared back at one another. Neither one of them wanted to say goodnight.

"Go on You Tube and find Freddy Jackson's *'I Could Use A Little Love Right Now.'* Listen to every word. Baby, you will hear it again on our wedding night," Ike stated before braving the cold night air.

He left her standing at the door with the cold wintry air cooling her down. She was still warm from his embrace and the feel of his lips on hers. After he pulled out the driveway, she went to her laptop to find the song. She liked it and listened to it several times before going to bed.

"Darling, I can use a little love right now," she sighed. "Grown folk's music, huh? I can't wait."

The next weekend Ike and Serena drove to Atlanta. Ikayla Joy's first visit with them was nothing short of another holiday. It was amazing how her little heart accepted both of them so quickly.

"Do you have a little girl?" Ikayla asked Serena, while swirling the spoon around in her banana split sundae.

"Not yet," Serena smiled. "When I marry your father I get to say that you're my little girl also. Is that okay? "

"Sure, my Mommy says that I have two moms, three grandfathers, three grandmothers, and a whole lot of aunts and cousins."

Evelyn, Serena, and Ike looked at each other with amusement. Ikayla Joy was full of questions.

"I warned you that she is quite inquisitive and articulate," Evelyn laughed.

"I'm glad that you're my daddy," Ikayla stated matter-of-factly, pushing her half empty ice cream bowl to the side.

"You are?" Ike smiled. "Why is that?"

"I think I kind of look just like you," she shrugged.

"I think you look like me too," Ike smiled. "Plus, you look like your Aunt Marlene and your two little cousins."

Ikayla's eyes lit up with excitement. "Can they come and play with me?"

"When you come visit me in Memphis you will get to play with them."

"Mommy, Mommy," Ikayla squealed happily, "Mr. Man said that I could come to his house to play. When Mommy? When can I go?"

Ike and Serena started laughing. "Wait a minute," Ike frowned. "You can't call me Mr. Man. Call me Daddy."

"Mommy said that I had to wait."

Ike looked at her sweet beautiful little round face. "You don't have to wait anymore. I'll be very sad if you don't call me Daddy."

"Daddy don't be sad," she stated, putting her little hand up to Ike's cheek. "You want some of my ice cream?"

Ike's heart melted inside. She was his flesh and blood. This was a love that he had never experienced before. His eyes misted with tears of joy.

"Oh my goodness," Evelyn laughed. "Daddy's little girl already. She's twisting him around her little fingers."

"That's right," Ike laughed. "She's my little girl and I'm her daddy."

Ike and Serena spent the rest of the afternoon alone with Ikayla shopping in the mall. Serena told Ikayla about the wedding plans and that she would be in the wedding party. Ikayla Joy easily bonded with her new daddy and mommy.

"Tell everybody that I'm the flower girl," she instructed Ike before saying goodbye.

"Okay," Ike replied, holding her in his arms for one last hug while kissing her on the cheek. He really wasn't ready to leave her. Their one day visit had gone too fast.

"See you later alligator," he stated in her ear.

"After while crocodile," she giggled, hugging him back.

"Sweetheart, you know that February 26th ends our 90 days of waiting," Ike grinned. "All of these extra wedding plans have just added on another 30 plus days."

"Aren't I worth the wait?" Serena pouted playfully. "The first Saturday in April is a good wedding date. I want the weather to be better. There is nothing nice about March winds and it's unpredictable forecasts."

"That makes it even better. Snuggling and baby making weather," Ike added.

Serena gave him a look. She didn't feel like talking about birth control and having children. Ike quickly changed the subject.

"So who's big idea was it to have this pre-Valentine's Day dinner tonight?"

"Your mother, the one and only, Mrs. Clarice Harper. You know she is cupid's best helper."

Serena and Ike had arrived first at the Butcher Block Steakhouse for dinner. Valentine's Day was two days away. Gladys had wanted to do something special and Clarice had agreed. Especially, since Ike and Serena were being so committed in keeping the amount of time they spent alone together under control.

"Well, what romantic plans could we possibly have made?" Serena asked, with a slight smirk.

Ike could sense her irritability. "What's got you so uptight? We should just let Pastor Kenton marry us and have a big reception. Then we can hurry up and get ourselves out of this misery and waiting."

The waitress had already seated them at a table for six. They sat quietly waiting for the others to arrive. Ike reviewed the wine list, while Serena watched as other people were seated. The lights were low and the candlelight flickered off of each table. A small jazz ensemble provided live entertainment. The atmosphere was cozy and romantic.

Ike put the menu away because he couldn't keep his eyes off Serena. She was looking more beautiful with each passing day. She had on a red and black figure fitting dress with a low neckline. He had noticed how it slid up her thighs when she got into his car. Her shapely legs looked slimmer. She had lost ten pounds. He was quick to let her know that there was no need to lose any more weight. Her hair had grown to shoulder length. She was roller setting it and letting it hang loosely. Her complexion was flawless. Her lips were painted red and she looked irresistible.

Serena was thinking the same thing about Ike. His low cut hair and wavy style looked good. She actually preferred it over his bald look but he liked his bald image better. He was wearing a red blazer and black open collared shirt. She admired the simple gold chain around his neck and the engagement band on his finger. Plus, his cologne was driving her insane.

"Are you two just going to sit there and stare at each other?" Clarice asked, approaching the table.

"Well, it's about time y'all got here," Ike replied. "We've been waiting for thirty minutes."

"We're sorry," Gladys replied. "Sam didn't realize that Walnut Grove had all that construction going on. We couldn't detour."

"Mother, you look lovely," Serena interrupted, standing to give Gladys a kiss. "Why are you not using your Hoveround? What's going on?"

"It's my gift to my sweetheart," she smiled. "Physical therapy has been good to me."

"She's feeling fast and prissy," Sam laughed. "Believe it when I say that we're taking it real slow."

"This is a real first class steakhouse," Mack Earl stated, enjoying the ambiance.

"Nothing but the best for us," Clarice grinned. "It's been a long time coming for me and you."

"Let's get this party started," Sam laughed.

They all ordered and listened to the jazz ensemble while waiting for their dinner. The conversation was good and everyone enjoyed a glass of wine. Mack Earl happily declined and ordered a glass of Ginger Ale on the rocks.

While everyone was enjoying the atmosphere and engaged in conversation, Serena was the first to notice an attractive and fashionably dressed woman approaching their table.

The woman looked like a celebrity and acted as though she knew them. The closer she got, Serena began to recognize her as Edgar Dupree's wife. Serena felt sick, weak, and nervous. Ike quickly detected the change in her demeanor.

"Serena, is that you?" the woman asked, approaching the table. "I just had to come and see. That engagement picture in the newspaper doesn't do you justice. I can see why you're my husband's pretty young thang."

Everyone at the table saw Serena's expression change from joy to despair. Ike's instinct to protect her quickly bolted him to his feet. But, Serena's gentle touch on his hand stopped him.

"Let her speak," Serena stated softly. She knew that there was no way out of this and that it was bound to happen in public or divorce court.

"Yeah, that's right, I'm the wife, Mrs. Edgar Dupree," she slurred, feeling tipsy from her vodka on the rocks. "I just wanted to introduce myself. Y'all looking so happy and in love over here."

Clarice was up for the confrontation. "Look Mrs. Dupree, if you want to talk about somebody's pretty young thang, you can step outside and discuss it with me."

Mrs. Dupree laughed loudly. "How charming! Indeed, you are a classy old dame, but my words are for this young engaged to be married couple."

Clarice could smell disaster. She knew exactly what was going to come up and out of this woman's mouth. She had been the receiver of many married women's accusations of being with their trifling and unfaithful husbands.

"Security! Security! We need security right now," Clarice yelled loudly, getting up from her chair. Mack Earl was right by her side calling for security also.

Mrs. Dupree took her opportunity and spoke loud and quick. "Little girl, you don't have to get married. You can have my so called husband. I only want his life insurance policy. And, I sure hope you don't have to share your man like I had to share mine with you and his other whores. Listen to me, Miss Pretty Young Thang, payback is hell. And by the way, I'll let your hunk of a man warm my bed any day or night. Let's just call it fair trade. You just stay the hell away from my husband. You little homewrecker."

Mrs. Edgar Dupree rushed off into the lobby area. The force of her words left everybody in awe. Serena's disturbed gaze followed her. She watched as Mrs. Dupree spoke to Edgar in the lobby and pointed in their direction. Edgar grabbed his wife by the arm and pushed her out the door.

"Breathe Clarice….breathe," Mack Earl spoke. "She ain't worth having no heart attack over and going to jail either."

Sam and Gladys were still dumbfounded from the words coming out the woman's mouth. There must have been some truth to it because Serena didn't offer any denial. She just sat there while Ike held her hand.

Security and the servers all showed up at the same time. They seemed to be uncertain as to what to do next.

"Serve the food," Sam stated anxiously.

"I think I'm going to step outside for a few minutes," Ike stated, releasing Serena's hand.

"No Ike, please don't," Serena pleaded softly.

"Serena, are you okay?" Gladys asked, reaching across the table to touch her hand.

Serena felt numb. The words had hurt, but at the same time they were liberating. Her dirty little secret was finally out in the open. Once again, she was in a bad script in a restaurant setting. But, this time a full cast were in the script with her, and everybody was playing their roles perfectly.

"She's okay," Ike responded. "Let's just eat our food. We can talk through this later."

"That's right," Sam stated. "The devil just wants to kill, steal, and destroy. We know his tricks, but he gets no victory here with us tonight."

Serena looked at her parents feeling ashamed and sorrowful. She could feel Ike squeezing her hand to offer support and encouragement.

"Mom and Dad, I didn't want you to find out like this. I didn't want you to find out through me being subpoenaed to court either. I'm kind of glad it's finally out in the opening. I'm just sorry for the way it happened."

"Darling, you don't have to explain," Gladys stated comfortingly. "Your father and I figured out your secret a long time ago."

"Ain't nothing new under the sun," Sam added. "Even scripture tells us that there is no temptation that is common to man. But, if we are faithful and just, God will provide a way of escape. All of us have sinned and fallen short. What's important is that you've repented and changed. We can only pray for them folks."

Serena stared lovingly at her family. Mack Earl and Clarice was just as understanding.

Serena gave a sigh of relief. "I was wondering if I would ever want to tell anybody about my sinful past but she's taken care of that. When God sent Ike my way, a way out was provided for me. I'm just sad for her. It makes me want to pray for both of them. They're in a living hell."

"Yeah, pray for 'em," Ike laughed. "I just want to say grace. So we can get back to our romantic evening."

"Waiter, bring another bottle of your best wine and Ginger Ale," Mack Earl yelled out, beckoning for the server. "And bring out those red roses that I stashed at the front desk. It's time for me to serenade these lovely ladies."

To everyone's surprise, Mack Earl went to the microphone. It didn't take them long to find his key and to play a recognizable Frank Sinatra tune.

"He's a natural and I think he's in the wrong business," Gladys stated to everyone.

"I know he's in the wrong business," Clarice laughed. "He's on the right path now that he has found me. And, I'm going to make sure he uses all of his talents."

They all lifted a glass of wine to toast Mack Earl. They listened while his smooth melodic voice added more ambiance to the evening.

L, is for the way you look at me.
O, is for the only one I see.
V, is very, very extraordinary.
E, is even more than anyone that you adore.
Love is all that I can give to you.
Love is more than just a game for two.
Two in love can make it.
Take my heart and please don't break it.
Love was made for me and you.

Early the next morning, Sam received an emotional phone call from Pastor Kenton. He couldn't quite understand his friend's words. But, he sensed that it was devastating from his deep sobs.

Pastor Kenton's voice was choked with emotions as he told Sam that his wife had died in her sleep. She had been the speaker for a Valentine's Dinner the night before. Marie was so overjoyed and they had such an exceptional evening. They came home and went to bed. She didn't wake up when he called her for breakfast.

Sam held the telephone. His mouth didn't say any words. He barely heard himself saying, "we're on the way."

Gladys felt as if someone had hit her with a ton of bricks when Sam broke the news to her as gently as he could. Through the years, Marie Kenton had become her closest friend.

"Oh Lord! She'll be calling me in a few minutes to tell me about last night. She was full of life and energy," Gladys cried loudly. "She had projects to be started and finished. She had visions and dreams of so many things to be done in the future. Oh Lord, my friend! Sam, is she really gone?"

Sam was pretty torn up too. "Marie always had a way of doing the right thing at the right time. It must have been her time. It was just something special about her."

His voice broke and he couldn't say anything else as he held Gladys in his arms. They cried together.

"Sam, I don't know, but I kind of think that she expected the end," Gladys stated tearfully. "The last few months she had a way of starting and stopping. Doing enough for you to get the idea of what to do. She said that she would finish it in the by-and-by. Oh, it'll get done is what she would say."

"Honey, come on and let's go see about our friend," Sam whispered. "He needs us."

"Yes he does," Gladys cried. "We all need each other right now. Lord, give us strength."

The mood was a somber one over the next few weeks. First Lady Kenton's passing had been a devastating blow to the Faith Baptist Church family. The realization that his wife would never be home again was hard for Pastor Kenton.  It was his deep faith and knowing that his wife was safe and secure in the arms of Jesus that gave him peace. Her transition was swift. He knew that Marie would not have wanted it any other way.

The month of April came and it was one day before Ike and Serena's wedding. Gladys was anxious to work in her rose garden. The meditational and therapeutic benefits would be good for her emotional healing. She was emotionally high with the wedding, but low in spirit while grieving for her friend.

Clarice sat Gladys down as a wedding planner with strict orders to just show up as the Mother of the Bride. She and Mack Earl would take over with the remaining plans. The wedding was at the church. The reception was being held at the same event center where she and Mack Earl were married. Unbeknownst to them all, Clarice and Mack Earl, were in agreement with the owner to buy and own the building for themselves.

"Baby, is this a dream? I can't believe that my ship has finally come in," Mack Earl stated, while they both signed the lease-purchase agreement for the event center.

"Believe it baby," Clarice beamed. "Both of our ships have come in. Our latter years will be our better years."

"Girl, you sounding like a good ol' church woman," Mack Earl laughed.

"That's right," she smiled. "And, I thank God, that I'm rightfully yoked together with a convert like yourself."

Mack Earl eyes misted with tears. "Ike and Serena's reception in our event center will be the talk of the town."

"Let's name it *Talk of the Town*," Clarice laughed.

"Let's pray about it," Mack Earl stated.

"Now, listen to you, sounding like a preacher. Look at what the Lord done did with our two wretched souls."

They both laughed. God had truly smiled on them.

During the rehearsal dinner, Pastor Kenton and Ike stepped outside in the night air. Since the funeral, Ike felt led to stay close to his pastor.

"Ike, I really appreciate your presence during this time. You've been such an inspiration to me. Plus, I have this strange desire to pour into you everything that I can about the Word and the business of the church."

"Sir, I have learned a lot under you. If you teach me anything else, I might end up in the pulpit with you."

"Oh Lord," Pastor Kenton smiled. "That will certainly be an answer to my prayer."

That statement fell like dead air. Ike showed no reaction. Pastor Kenton continued to talk.

"Ike, I've only shared this with Sam, but I want you to know firsthand. I will be resigning and moving back to

North Carolina. Our children and family are there. It's just best for my future."

Ike was truly surprised. "Wow, this is breaking news! When will you do this?"

"By the end of May. My oldest daughter is traveling with me to the Holy Land. I've wanted to take this trip for a long time. So, the Official Board will need to appoint a search committee, and I'm hoping that you will be on that committee."

"Am I needed? Are there guidelines? Is there a procedures manual?" Ike questioned.

"Of course, you're needed. Anybody that's young and with fresh insight is needed. Those old buzzards haven't had to find a pastor in twenty years. They're all just as old as me. This church has a chance to break some traditional strongholds and meet the needs of this generation. A few women are needed on the committee also."

"Pastor, I see your point," Ike replied. "This is going to require a whole lot of prayer."

"Fasting too," Pastor Kenton added.

A few minutes later and without any warning a gentle rain began to fall.

"This is not good," Ike grimaced, looking toward the sky. "The rain isn't supposed to come until next week."

Pastor Kenton welcomed the rain by lifting his hands in praise. His eyes misted with tears.

"My Marie loved the rain," he wept. "God is letting me know that she is with Him. I can hear her saying…, *"When it rains on your parade to look up because without the rain there would be no rainbow. Into each life a little rain must fall. Your tears can wash your soul like rain."* Yes indeed, she had a way of saying things."

Ike stood with Pastor Kenton as the raindrops from heaven fell down on both of them. Just as soon as the rain had started — it stopped suddenly.

"April showers bring May flowers," Ike laughed. "It's probably going to do this all day tomorrow. I just hope the bride and our mothers can deal with it without more wedding day stress."

Pastor Kenton smiled. "They'll be alright. We all know that God never promised us days without pain and laughter, and sun without rain. But, he did promise strength for our souls and that will see us through."

"Amen," Ike agreed. "Pastor, he's definitely given you strength for your soul."

The first Saturday in April had finally arrived. The wedding was set for four o'clock and it was a beautiful day.

Serena watched from the living room window of her parent's home as the wedding guests arrived at the church. She  was dressed and waiting for her father to come and escort her across the street when it was time for her entrance.

There were no bridesmaids and groomsmen. Only Ikayla Joy and their parents made up the wedding party. Serena had made an abrupt decision to keep it small and simple after her last altercation with Dimples. Although, Dimples stated that she was happy for them, Serena's intuition told her different.

"Dimples, why can't you come to the bridal shower?" Serena asked her friend. "You will already be in town and the rehearsal dinner is the next day."

"It's a lingerie shower and I'm not feeling it. Couldn't you have come up with something for everybody to enjoy?"

"Dimples, I'm just not into male strippers and poll dancing," Serena laughed.

"Well, giving you lingerie to be sashaying around Ike and talking happy homemaker crap is certainly not my ideal bridal shower."

Serena was stunned at Dimple's remarks. For a few minutes, neither one of them said a word.

"You're jealous...just plain jealous!" Serena heard herself saying to Dimples.

"Because I'm truthful that makes me jealous," Dimples snapped back. "I'm just not a hypocrite and someone who acts like they're a saint."

Serena could feel her heart breaking. Dimples' true feelings were finally coming out.

"Is that what you think about me?"

Dimples didn't hesitate. "Yes, I think you are role playing. You act like you've been a saint and that you have never done anything un-Christian in your entire life. "

Serena could feel her temper beginning to boil. It was time to end this conversation.

"Dimples, I can't be anybody but me," Serena stated. "I'm not going to let you or anyone else hold my sins over my head. I repented, God forgave me, and I'm free. Plus, he blessed me with a husband to call my own."

"Oh really!" Dimples laughed. "Well, be careful my friend. What goes around can come back around and you know firsthand what I mean. Girl, I live in the real world. You reap what you sow and payback is hell. "

After that conversation, Serena knew she had to cut her ties with Dimples. She doubted if their friendship would ever be the same again. Maybe, God was telling her something, and she certainly had enough sense to take it for its true meaning. She discussed it with Ike and they both agreed that they didn't need or want the drama.

"One bad apple don't spoil a whole wedding party," Clarice stated. "What about the other people who are happy and excited about being in the wedding?"

"I just want to keep it simple," Serena stated. "Anyway, the wedding party was getting too large. It's not too late for me to let them know that I've changed my mind. They'll be okay with it."

"Dimples sounds like a woman scorned," Mack Earl shouted from the next room.

"My exact sentiments," Serena shouted back.

Clarice smiled at her future daughter-in-law. "I've always known that you were the woman for Ike. Dimples was trouble from the start and she'll be trouble in the future. Keep your guard up with her. She's the kind that can't accept rejection on any level. I know her type well."

"Well, she better go and find her own husband because she can't have mine," Serena stated smugly.

"Now, that's what I'm talking about and that's the right attitude to have," Clarice smiled.

The insistent ringing from the telephone snapped Serena back into the present. It was fifteen minutes before show time. She was certain that it was Ike calling.

"Ike, what do you want?" she laughed.

There was no response. Just silence on the other end.

"Hello….hello. Who is this?" Serena inquired.

"You don't have to do this. We can still be together," stated the voice on the other end.

Serena's heart dropped to her feet. It was Edgar Dupree and he was calling on her wedding day. She couldn't believe what her ears were hearing. Her voice failed her.

Edgar sounded desperate. "Baby, the divorce is final. I ended the marriage. She's an alcoholic. Baby, you can marry me now. We can be together. Don't do it!"

Serena felt sorry for him. "Edgar, go away. I never loved you. I thought I did but it wasn't love. I know what love is now. God has given me a husband that I can call my own. I'm going to pray for you and your family."

"Pray for yourself. I'm coming to the wedding," Edgar laughed. "Plus, I'm going to send a fire truck to the church in a few minutes. You must have forgotten who you are dealing with. I enforce the law when and how I choose."

"Oh, I know exactly who you are," Serena shouted loudly. "You're the devil! And you have no power over me anymore! I rebuke you! Get behind me Satan!"

Serena hung up the phone. She was shocked. After a few minutes she could feel herself returning to normal. She had never felt so free in her life. She couldn't wait to tell Ike what had just happened. Together, they were going to stomp that devil Edgar Dupree out of their lives.

She admired her appearance in the full-length mirror. Instead of a long gown she had chosen to wear a vintage white lace tea length wedding dress. Her shimmering stockings and white satin heels completed her attire. Her veil was short and fashionable with a beautiful brocade of roses and pearls. She wore it tilted to one side slightly covering her face with a matching bridal bouquet. Her curls were stylishly loose and flowing.

The sound of Samuel Garrett coming through the front door was a welcomed delight. "Baby girl, are you ready?" he smiled, admiring her from across the room. "Your groom is willing, ready, and anxious."

"Daddy, you look so handsome!"

"I clean up pretty good don't I?" Sam laughed.

"Daddy, it's about to happen. I'm getting married!"

Sam stretched out his arm and Serena embraced her father. "God has answered all of our prayers. He's done more than we could have ever imagined. I'm so proud of you and Ike. God's blessings have come in like a flood."

They were both tearing up. "Oh no," Serena sighed. "We're not going to do this. My makeup is too perfect."

"Tell your mother that because she's over their crying her eyes out. Clarice is grinning like a Chess cat. Ikayla Joy has been down the aisle twice throwing rose buds. And, Mack Earl is having a one man's solo show."

"Come on Dad, we better hurry before Ike comes bursting through the door."

"I think you're right about it," Sam laughed.

Several hours later, Ike and Serena left the reception while the party was still going strong. Clarice had provided the limousine driver a list of things to do before the newlyweds could enter the condo.

Ike and Serena waited patiently while the driver unloaded all the wedding gifts and took care of his checklist. When he had finished, he verified his return time in three days to transport them to the airport for a two week stay in Hawaii.

Ike led his bride into their home. The last week before the wedding he had stayed at Clarice's house while she and Gladys added their final touch to the condo. He was anxious as Serena to see the condo, and both of them were pleasantly surprised.

The glow from candle lights, soft music, and the smell of fresh flowers greeted them. There was champagne on ice, chocolate covered strawberries, and a tray of delightful hors d'oeuvres set up in the dining area. A trail of rose petals lead to the kitchen. The refrigerator had been stocked with wine coolers, juices, sodas, bottled water, and an assortment of edible delights. They followed another trail of rose petals that led to the master bedroom.

"Let's save this room for last. I want you to see the other rooms," Ike stated.

"Oh Ike, this place looks wonderful. You've done a lot since I was last here."

"Fresh paint and new carpet for my bride is only right. We'll buy our new place together but this is home for now."

"It's perfect," Serena stated, feeling overjoyed.

Ike's office had been redone. Two contemporary office desks faced each other. One desk held Ike's personal computer and the other a brand new IMac desktop computer. One bookcase was filled and the other bookcase was empty. There were two file cabinets in the closet with bins for storage and supplies.

"Is the Macintosh for me?" Serena squealed.

"You're the only Mac user I know. My only request for sharing this office is that you don't distract me. I do some serious studying and I'm sure you will be a distraction."

Serena was feeling very aroused. She stepped out of her heels and slowly begin to untie Ike's bowtie.

"I think distractions should happen anywhere and in anyway necessary. Especially when appreciation is being shown. That's how I feel about distractions."

Ike quickly grabbed her by the hand and led her to the next room. "Let's speed up this walkthrough," he laughed, feeling more than a little anxious for their last stop.

The next room was the bedroom that had been prepared for Ikayla Joy. There was one twin-sized bed with a decorative strawberry pink and yellow comforter set accessorized with stuffed teddy bears. The room also provided extended closet space and a dressing area for Serena. The two closets were filled with her shoes and clothing. Unpacked boxes lined the dresser and chest.

"I see they left these boxes for me," Serena laughed. "Ikayla and I are going to love this room. It's perfect for us."

Ike had started taking off his cuff links and unbuttoning his shirt. Serena could feel his eyes slowing undressing her. Excitement, anticipation, and a sensuous rhythm was building up in both of them. She purposely continued her walkthrough into the newly decorated full-sized bathroom in the hallway. Ike stood patiently at the master bedroom door awaiting her arrival.

"Mrs. Harper, I could use a little love right now," he stated huskily. "It's time."

Serena walked into his waiting and open arms. No words were spoken. Their eyes, roaming hands, and passionate kisses were communicating their desires and needs. Ike slowly began to undo her pinned up hairstyle. She rubbed her hands under his open shirt. He unzipped her dress and unfastened all barriers that kept his flesh from touching her flesh.

"Ike....my gown...your tuxedo...we should hang them up," she stated softly between his tender kisses.

"We should consummate this marriage," he stated, while opening the door. "Everything else can wait."

Soft candlelight filled the room. The bed was covered with white satin sheets and scattered with red rose petals. Another champagne bucket stand was next to the bed with two gold plated flutes.

"Wow," Serena smiled. "They laid it out."

"Yep, even they know what's going down in here tonight," Ike stated.

He picked up the remote to his sound system and queued up Freddy Jackson's song. "I told you that you would hear it again," he whispered huskily in her ear.

Serena closed her eyes as Ike's body joined with hers. They both surrendered to each other completely. They had truly become one in spirit and in body as Freddie Jackson's melodic voice saturated the atmosphere with their song.

"Darlin' I, I could use a 'lil love right now. Come on, come on, give it to me. Darlin' I, I could use a 'lil love right now. Whenever we touch like this, whenever I kiss your lips, baby my heart beats faster by the minute. Whenever I touch your face, you know I want you right here. I want you right now, cause there's so much pleasure in your embrace. Darlin' I, I could use a 'lil love right now. Darlin' I, I could use a 'lil love right now. Do it in the bath, do it in the tub. Do it in the living room on the rug. Do it in the kitchen, do it in the sink. Do it whichever way you think. Darlin I, I could use a 'lil love right now."

The newlyweds spent the next forty-eight hours in a honeymoon bliss. Neither one of them had ever experienced happiness at this level. Everything about their life felt new and exciting. Each day that they awoke together was a day of joy. They had no idea how complete marriage would make them feel. It was simply surreal.

"I think this is how Adam and Eve must have felt," Ike stated, sitting across from Serena in their home office. "I ain't never felt nothing like this before in my whole entire life."

"I know," Serena agreed lovingly. "Ike, we've become one now. Isn't it amazing?"

"It's more than amazing! Was it worth the wait?"

Serena's eyes revealed her answer. "I never doubted that you lacked in pleasing a woman."

"I never doubted your skills either," Ike grinned. "Obviously you were doing something right to keep you know who coming back for four years. A sweet little church girl like you...shame on you."

Serena laughed out loud. It didn't surprise her at all that Ike would mention her past.

"Look who's talking, with your love 'em and leave 'em self. We certainly were not virgins. I only hope that you can surpass what I've grown accustomed to experiencing."

"See, you're a fast 'lil ol' something," Ike laughed. He liked the fact that she was open and didn't have a problem expressing her desires and feelings.

"Baby, baby, baby, I'm going to rock your world for the rest of your life. I'm all the woman that you will ever need."

"And I'm all the man that you will ever need."

"Ike, I pray that we don't go outside of our marriage bed to be fulfilled and satisfied."

Ike could hear the sincerity in her voice. Her request was coming from personal experience.

"Baby, let's promise to always be open and communicate our true feelings and sexual needs. That way we'll know if we're at risk."

"That's a promise," Serena smiled. She left her desk and came over to sit on his lap.

"See, this is exactly what I mean by distractions," Ike laughed, encircling her into his arms.

"Husband, what are you writing?"

Ike was finally ready to share his writings. "Baby, I've been working on this since we made our commitment to be abstinent. I'm hoping to teach it to the youth and young adults, if you're in agreement."

Serena was moved to tears as she began to read her husband's writings from the computer screen.

"ABSTAIN, with teachings on each letter," she read.

"It sure is," Ike smiled. "Serena, this thing has been working with me. I have scriptural reference for each letter. This is what kept me going and gave me the strength that I needed. I know God wants us to teach it to others. Our mess is our message and our testing is our testimony."

Serena was overwhelmed. "Oh Ike, it's beautiful and I would love to tell and teach this message with you. This is definitely divine."

"It can use a little tweaking. But, I figure each person can create their own meaning as it pertains to them. This is how it ministered to me."

"It captures both of us perfectly."

Ike pulled her into his arms and they held each other tight. "Are you happy?" he asked softly.

"Insane and crazy happy," she smiled, snuggling closer to him. "Ike, I can finally tell the world that I have a husband to call my own, and that he is a God-sent husband."

"And, I too, can say I have a wife to call my own, and that she is a God-sent wife."

"I can't wait to get to Hawaii," Serena smiled.

"Two whole weeks in paradise," Ike grinned.

"I doubt if we'll get bored and run out of things to do."

"I think we got that covered," Ike laughed. "Let the church say Amen!"

Ike's Acronym

Absolutely

Believing

Standing

Truthful

Anointed *and*

Indwelling *in*

Newness

Discussion Guide
A Husband To Call My Own

How many of us knowingly get ourselves into sinful situations?

Why and what are some reasons that a person(s) become involved in affairs and promiscuous lifestyles?

Discuss how deception, secrecy, and lies can be painful and hurting to relationships, families, and loved ones.

Discuss why Serena stayed in the relationship for so long. Are these types of break-ups easier said than done?

Is Ike's portrayal of his mother and their lifestyle something that we find prevalent in homes and families?

Is it possible that Ike fell in love with Serena at first sight? How important is it to differentiate between love and lust?

Discuss Serena and Dimples' conversations about Ike. Was it likely that their friendship would encounter friction? Why? Discuss Ike and Dimples' friendship.

Clarice and Mack Earl lives are changed. How realistic is it that relationships like theirs develop into marriage?

How idealistic is it that the "Church" can be the connector for dating and looking for a spouse?

Discuss how Faith Baptist Church is modeling evangelism and outreach?

Discuss abstinence. Why is it so difficult? Is old-fashioned courting/courtships obsolete?

Do couples honestly engage in real talk about their past partners and lifestyles? How important is it that couples discuss their health and medical histories?

Marlene shares the problems in her marriage. How common is her situation in this day and time? As the body of Christ, are we open, perceptive, and ministering to these types of problems and situations?

In the restaurant scene, what are the chances and realities of the wife confronting the other woman? Could it have played out differently?

What do you think about Ike and Pastor Kenton's relationship? Do you agree the Kenton's marriage is also a model for Ike and Serena? If so, how?

Discuss Edgar's phone call on the wedding day. What are the chances of something like that really happening? What could Serena have done differently?

Discuss Ike and Serena's feelings after the consummation of their marriage. Do you agree this is how God intended it to be? Are they off to a good start by discussing being faithful and honoring their marital bed?

Discuss Ike's acronym. Is this something that needs teaching in today's society? Do you think that Christian believers can start a new trend with this mindset in dating and marriage?

Bonus Question. Can you see a second book and storyline for the continuation of these characters? What are they? If so, contact me at brenda@brendajoycenichols.com